A Lil' Less Broken

Book One
The Kingsmen MC Series

Tara Oakes

First edition. July 16, 2014

Written by Tara Oakes
Published by Kindle Direct Publishing
Book Cover: Image from Tatiana Villa,
www.viladesign.net
TO MY LAMBCHOP, MY LOVE

ALSO FROM THIS AUTHOR:

A LIL' LESS LOST, Book two in the Kingsmen MC series

A LIL' LESS HOPELESS, Book three in the Kingsmen MC series

BITTER SWEET DECEPTION, Book four in the Kingmen MC series

BABY V, Book one in the Chianti Kisses series

BOSS, Book two in the Chianti Kisses series

ALL AVAILABLE NOW ON AMAZON.COM

ACKNOWLEGMENTS

A LIL' LESS BROKEN, Book one in the Kingsmen MC series, was my very first written book. I had no idea what I was doing when the publish button was pressed. All I has was a story in my head that wanted to be told. Since then, the Kingsmen have taken on a life of their own.

Thanks so much to all the readers who have embraced this series. This book was written long before the days of my PA, Alicia, long before Des, my street team, my fan base.

These are some of the people who are now indispenseable to me, and without whom each of the following books would not be possible. So, I'm giving a huge thanks to everyone who has helped the Kingsmen become what they have.

BIKER FRIENDLY REFERENCE

The life of a biker although foreign to most of us, is a very intriguing subculture with its own laws, rules, language, and traditions. Hopefully this reference will help the rest of us get to know a bit more about them before we take a peak into the lives of Lil's and Jay, two people born and raised in the secret world of the MC, full of passion, loyalty, fierce family bonds and... danger.

TERMS

1%er -
The small population of biker clubs that consider themselves outside the law. They often run operations in gambling, guns, prostitution, smuggling, paid protection, drugs, and more. They are considered to be the baddest of the bad, and the roughest of the rough.

Brother -
Club members within the same club refer to each other as 'Brother'. They have made a vow to each other to protect and take care of each other as family.

Cage-
An automobile, usually a van.

Church –
A club meeting to be attended by patched brothers only. Most clubs run as a democracy and important matters are voted on during meetings.

Club Mama –
Women that regularly attend events and interact with the M.C. They may aspire to become an Ol' lady one day but do not yet have a patch holder. They may spend time with many different bikers within a club but have loyalty to the club first before a man. They are considered to be a little bit more respected than a sweet butt.

Cut -
Refers to the leather vest worn by most bikers in a club.

M.C.-
Acronym for Motorcycle Club.

Ol' Lady –
A term of affection used for the main woman, or wife, of a club member. She is given his protection and is considered off limits to any other biker. Women are not considered club members, but rather have associations to the club through their Ol' man, or their patch holder.

Nomad –
A member of an MC that is currently without a specific charter. They are still considered a brother but they choose not to offer specific allegiance to a designated charter, instead they are loyal to the club organization in whole.

Patched In –
When a prospect completes his initiation period and is voted in to become a full fledged club member, or "Brother"

Patches –
The cloth patches or embroidered designs added to a biker's vest, or cut, that identifies which club they belong to, the location of their specific charter and their position in it. Other patches can be added to signify milestone events. Example: if the member has ever served prison time for his club, or killed for it.

Piece –
A gun.

Prospect –
Those that desire to become a full-fledged patched member must complete an initiation period as a

prospect before a final vote is taken as to whether or not they can fully join. Prospect's usually are given the worst assignments and must prove their loyalty and worth to the club.

Rag –
Another term for a leather vest, or cut, but worn by a woman, given to her by her Ol' man to signify that she is his "property" and is off limits. An Ol' lady's rag does not usually bear the club name, logo or charter as she is not a club member. It simply states "Property of_____"

Sweet Butt –
A term used to describe a woman who is used by members in a club. They are usually welcomed to club parties, or "Brother only" parties but are never allowed at family events. It is a derogatory term and there is very little respect for these ladies by club members.

Tat –
A tattoo. Full fledged club members, or brothers, often have the club patches permanently tattooed on their body to signify that they are a member even if not wearing their cuts. An Ol' lady will usually have a tattoo to honor her Ol' man to signify that she is his property even if she is not wearing her rag.

CHAPTER ONE

SATURDAY

This is bad. This is so fucking bad. I can't believe this is actually happening. I must have the worst damn luck. If my left cheek wasn't throbbing so much, I could pass this all off as a dream.

The sun is rising higher in the morning sky. If I had to guess, it's probably going on 8 AM, maybe 9. I haven't slept in thirty hours, but sleep deprivation is the least of my worries, adrenaline still coursing through me, keeping the fatigue at bay. What is taking so long? I know enough about this crap to know that I should either be dead, or worse by now. I lift my eyes to scan the men keeping a watchful eye over me, and decide that death will be my choice.

The man closest to me reeks of beer and body odor. His tattoos are large and faded... skulls, thorns, chicks with big tits... yada yada yada. The same cliché ink that most of these guys are sporting. His large black boots are covered in dirt and worn. I glance up, taking stock as I go. Dirty jeans, splattered with blood, mud and who knows what else. Prince Charming notices my rising eyes and grabs his crotch, thrusting his hips toward me.

"You see something you want, girlie?" he spits as he gyrates to me. Bile forms in my throat, and I gulp down my disgust.

"Nahhh... I'm good." *This is REALLY fucking bad.* Ok. I need to think of my options. No one knows I'm here. I was supposed to sneak into town last night, meet up with Christine and some girls for her bachelorette party and then clear out first thing this morning before anyone caught wind that I was back. I should have known better. If Christine hadn't been my closest friend since childhood, I would have stayed away. Options. What the hell are my options, here?

The roar of motorcycles quickly approaching practically gives me whiplash as my head jerks up to see. Great. Well, at least I don't have to worry about options anymore. I won't be needing them. It's now out of my hands.

I watch as the bikes clear past me, sitting on an old wooden picnic bench in the middle of the fenced in lot. I count each one, as an invisible knife slowly tears at my gut with each passing Harley. The first, carries a huge man bearing the nastiest scowl I have ever seen, partially hidden by dark sunglasses. His black leather vest covers his matching t-shirt. I can't be more than thirty feet away, but I don't need to squint and try to read the words in patches and embroidery on his cut. I know them by heart.

Vince, my Godfather, is nothing to mess with. I've known a lot of rough guys in my life but he tops the cake. As the president of the Kingsmen MC he is respected for that roughness, having earned every bit of it. He can also be a teddy bear, although I seriously doubt that I'll be seeing that side of him today.

If Vince had come alone, I could probably have handled it. The immense feelings of disappointment and shame might be manageable if it was only him that came to my rescue today. But no, I have no fucking luck remember? The whole Goddamned cavalry had to come instead.

I resolve myself to the inevitable amount of shit that is about to come down on me, as I watch Vince dismount his Harley, followed by my dad Butch, my brother Tiny, and my "uncles" Chaps, Dewey and Clink. The last rider stays on his bike, staring at me. My breathing hitches as I lock eyes with him. There are no emotions in those eyes at the moment, although I had seen enough to last me a lifetime.

Tiny strides past Vince and nearly reaches me before my lovely groin-grabbing captor blocks his path.

"Untie her fuckin' hands right now you fuckin' bastard!" Tiny screams at the man who I have nicknamed "Crotch" for the time being.

Vince and my dad grab his shoulders back restraining him from tearing the other guy's head clean off. Vince holds him back as he stares down "Crotch" with invisible daggers. He speaks out to Tiny without breaking eye contact with my guard.

"Not here brother... we handle this inside with Shade." He softens his voice but not his gaze, "You OK Lil's? You hurt at all?," he asks out to me.

Besides the throbbing in my left cheek from being backhanded, the ropes cutting into my wrists and the splinters poking into my ass from the ancient table beneath, not to mention lack of clothing (I had been to a bachelorette party after all), I'd say I was in pretty good shape. Clamping my knees together, suddenly aware of my abundance of bare flesh, I blush and whisper my answer.

"Never been better." The sarcasm isn't lost on any of us.

The lingering rider finally dismounts his bike, placing his helmet on the handlebar, and calls out.

"Enough of this bullshit. Let's fuckin' do this already." He has such an air of authority about him, that even I can't help but fall in line. His sandy brown hair has that disheveled, recently mussed look to it. What I wouldn't give to run my fingers through that hair right now, pull it down close to me......

"You." He finally breaks his stare from mine and addresses my newfound, pelvic-obsessed friend. He snaps his fingers as he points to my wrists tied together, resting in my lap. "Untie her now."

Turning on his heel, he stalks away into the building behind him. Vince and my dad push Tiny in the same direction and follow through the doorway. With all the shit that has gone down in the last twelve hours, I am not prepared to see him. Not now, not like this.

Jasper was my first love, my only love. I haven't seen him in two years and the first glimpse he sees of me is tied, all slutted up, and in a shit-storm of trouble. Great. This day cannot possibly get any fucking worse.

******

At least an hour must have passed. I sit rubbing my wrists to try and quiet the stinging. The dirtbags hovering around me have since backed off, giving me a little breathing room. This is torture, sitting here with nothing to do but think of Jasper, or "Jay" as the club calls him. Nothing but minute after minute to think about how much I loved him, needed him and hated him. He was everything I wanted, everything I craved. He also broke my heart and crushed my soul along with it. I guess you could say that's where this whole damn mess started.

He was young, I was younger. It could have been called fate. We grew up together, born and raised in the MC. We always knew that he would patch in when he was old enough. He and Tiny patched in together. It was a really proud moment for our family, like passing the torch to the next generation. Our dad's were so pleased that their boys would carry on the tradition, and the

15

club that they built with their own bare hands would live on in the sons.

I had always had a crush on Jay. He was the drop-dead gorgeous older boy who had swagger dripping out of his pores. I wasn't the only one to notice, either. He was never shy with the girls and he and Tiny always had tramps and sluts hanging all over them. I was the annoying younger sister that they never wanted around. After several years of being told to scram off, or one too many pranks pulled on me, I gave them their space and started to grow up on my own.

I never quite fit in with the girls my age. They were into Barbie dolls, makeup, boy bands and shopping. I was into sports, books and school. I always kept my grades up and had one or two boys from class interested in me. That never lasted long though, as Tiny and Jay would always find a way to scare them off.

THEN

When I turned sixteen, something changed. Not suddenly or out of nowhere, but gradually. Jay started to pop up randomly when Tiny wasn't around. He was twenty-three and had just patched into the MC as a full member. I hadn't seen him much during the couple of years that they were prospecting to get into the club... I'm sure they were kept busy with club bullshit and nonsense.

16

He was so hot, and older, and experienced, and tough. I was none of those things and naturally drawn to him like a moth to a flame. He was strong and I felt safe and protected by him. He called me baby and I would just melt into his blue eyes. Butch wasn't thrilled that we were spending so much time together. I was always warned to keep my grades up and that nothing would be getting in the way of going to college. Especially not some "hot shot, little shit that wanted in my pants." Yeah, dad was a real poet.

After a couple of weeks, I noticed that all of the boys starting to avoid me, even the one or two that could always be counted on to ask me to see a movie on the weekend or study for a test together. I'm sure seeing the older, tough as nails biker dropping me off in the morning and picking me up every afternoon didn't help matters much. It didn't take long until Jay was hanging around field hockey practice and showing up to games, even our travel ones.

When a month or so had passed I started to get the impression that maybe I wasn't imagining the hot, thick, tension between us. Maybe it wasn't just a kid sister protectiveness, maybe it was something more. Any doubts I had were quelled one night at a charter party back at the MC's clubhouse. It wasn't unusual for me to be there, considering both my brother and my pop were patched members. Jay stayed by my side the entire night.. critiquing my pool shot, sneaking me cups of

17

beer instead of soda. By the time I would usually leave these parties... you know... when the brothers would pair off with their lays for the night and the clubhouse started to resemble the set of a porn flick, Jay grabbed my hand and led me to the roof of the main building, far away from and out of earshot of the moaning and all out debauchery downstairs.

We lay side by side on the sloping roof, staring up at the clear night. It never got too cold in Chisolm, South Carolina... especially on a warm May night like that one, but suddenly I started to shiver. Jay pulled me close, noticing my shaking,

"Shhhh... baby... you cold?"

I wasn't cold. But, somehow it seemed like the right thing to do to agree with him. Especially if it meant that he would be holding on to me to warm me with his steamy body heat. Jay smelled so good. Being that close to him I became enveloped in his soapy clean muskiness. He rubbed my shoulders and then my arms, trying to warm me from my "chill." The heat from the friction soon spread over me, flushing my face and neck and plummeting to my core. I had never felt anything like that before and could only compare it to the feeling one might get from a free falling elevator. Responding to these intense sensations, my body started to squirm slightly, searching for some type of anchor to calm the chaos.

Jay tucked his chin into the crook behind my ear and whispered in a raspy, husky voice, "That better, babe?"

His lips lingered and explored the sensitive skin, breathing deep into my flowing hair. My eyes began to flutter and I held my breath afraid of what would escape if I tried to answer.

When I didn't respond for several moments, Jay pressed on my shoulders pulling me to him while rolling himself slightly over, hovering and placing his hands on either side, while lifting himself directly above. With only an inch or so between us, he stared into me and locked my gaze with his. I could feel the breath from his lips come onto mine as he spoke.

"I'm not gonna play around with this anymore, babe. You my girl?"

My eyes widened, taking in the full weight of his words. His Girl? How could I be his girl? I'm still sixteen... for another few weeks, anyway. I'm the annoying little brat that they used to play tricks on and tease until I ran crying to mom, or Jay's mom. He was twenty-three, gorgeous, and a real bad-ass. What did he need a girl for? I mean it was nothing he couldn't get anytime he wanted from the Club Mama's hanging around every night, or the Sweet Butts that came slinking in for parties.

I could feel my breath quickening and my pulse racing. Jay's hips slowly started moving down onto mine and settled their full weight between my thighs, then a slight bit of pressure started pressing into me. He hadn't blinked once. He just stared into me as my eyes raced around and my shallow, labored breathing tried its damnedest to regulate itself. He brought his lips on top of mine, brushing their plumpness delicately over mine.

"I asked.... are you my girl?"

Heat soared down to my legs and raced around into my stomach. My breathing finally slowed and I answered in the best way I could, "I don't know.... am I?"

Jay seemed to like my response. His eyes flickered a hint of mischief and then hooded themselves.

"Damn right you're my girl..." He crashed his lips down on top of mine. I arched my neck up to meet him as his lips surrounded mine and pressed into them, onto them and around them. My mouth was putty in his as he guided me expertly deeper together. His lips parted slightly and I felt his moistness urging me to follow his lead. I had kissed a boy before, (well two if you counted Joey McDonough in the seventh grade) but this was different. This was kissing a man.

His tongue powerfully stroked my lips, first my top lip and then just as strong on my lower, urging them to open further for him. I followed his unspoken directions and allowed him to enter into me, searching for my own tongue and the comfort it would give him. He swirled around, thrusting in, exploring what was hidden inside, maneuvering mine to match his rhythm. He tasted just as good as he smelled. A bit smoky, a bit spicy and a helluva lot like a deep musk would taste.

He growled lightly, pulling me closer to him, as he pressed deeper onto me. The hardness of his manhood throbbing against my thigh through our jeans. I suddenly panicked... never venturing this far into passion with a boy before, I was certain my inexperience would start to show and Jay would realize what a child I was compared to the slutty Club Mama's that knew how to satisfy him without pause. I started to inch my face away and tense myself.

Jay pulled himself away from my lips and pressed his forehead to mine, seeming to strain against himself.

"Baby... you have no idea how much I love how innocent you are." He kissed my closed lips softly once more, "You're mine. My girl. No one else's. Say it baby."

"I'm your girl".

NOW

The door to the clubhouse of the Slayers MC finally opens as if answering my silent prayers. Thank God. I need this to be over with already. The waiting and the suspense are killing me. The last thing I need at this point is more time to think back and remember the details of my very own shattered biker-fairytale. I lived it, hell I've relived it a thousand times. The last thing I wanted was to remember....

Clink, Chaps and Dewey march out first, soon followed by my dad and my brother. They come right to me, offering me a bottle of cold water and a large Kingsmen t-shirt to cover my trashy midriff top. My pop grabs hold of me and squeezes tightly.

"Baby girl what the hell were you thinking?!" He scowls at me. Before I can answer, he pulls me in tight, rocking slightly back and forth, offering whatever little bit of fatherly comfort he can.

"I don't know pop. It all happened so fast. Everything just got out of hand. How did you know I was here?"

I had never been so thankful to see my Dad, but unless his fatherly radar was working overtime he shouldn't have had any reason to think that I was anywhere other than in my apartment three hours away in River Rapids. Tiny strokes my hair back from my face as I cradle into my dad's shoulder and answers for him.

"Your friend Christina came to the clubhouse and told Jay. We geared up and set a meeting with Shade to squash this shit. Jay and Vince are working out the details now."

My pop finally lets me out of his bear hug and inspects me, "You hurt girl? These sons of bitches do anything to you?"

There is an unspoken meaning to his questioning. The Slayers have a nasty reputation when it comes to women, from what I've been able to pick up over the years. Shade, their president had even served time for it. All the girls in town know to stay away from them. I understand what my dad is asking.

"No pop. I'm fine. I just need to get out of here and go home."

I lied. If I even so much as hinted that the big burly bald guy in the back of us had backhanded me last night I know it would be an all out shit-storm.

Butch nods to me and cups my chin. The entire group turns our attention once more to the clubhouse door as Shade, Vince and Jay step out into the sunlight. Jay already has his sunglasses on, making it more than difficult to read anything from him. Vince shakes hands awkwardly and stiffly with Shade, mouthing something I can't make out. Shade smirks at the comment and calls out to his goons.

"Boys, it appears our hospitality has been appreciated. Our guests will be leaving now. All of them." I exhale. That last bit was an obvious reference about me. "Jay," Shade calls out as Jasper follows Vince towards us. "Seventy two hours".

I look around from Butch to Clink, to Dewey, Chaps and finally Tiny, to reassure myself that it is really over. "Thank God. Thank you all so much. Can I really go home now?"

Vince makes his way next to me and kisses my cheek. The others allow him to answer.

"Lil's... We're going home." I close my eyes tight, the stress of last night finally getting the best of me. I bite my lip to hold back my tears. Vince squeezes my shoulder reassuringly before he adds, "You're riding with your Ol' man," before he and all of the other Kingsmen seek out their bikes.

My body suddenly feels as if it weighs a thousand pounds. Shock sets in as I register Vince's words.

"Wait... *MY WHAT?!*" I call out behind them as I search each of them for a visible answer. My heart stops when I finally set eyes on Jay as he straddles over his bike, staring forward, away from me, and holds out his own helmet as if it were poison and he wants nothing more than to drop it.

"Get on," he growls.

My mouth dries. No way... this can't be happening. Jay stands stone still, not letting the helmet waiver one bit as I stand in shock. "I said... GET ON. NOW. "

I frantically look to my brother and my pop to step in and end this... whatever this is. They look down, away, anywhere they can but at me. They start their engines and fall in line with Vince, waiting to leave. I can see Jay getting pissed off. Fearing he'll take off without me, I walk over to his outstretched arm, taking the helmet from him.

I strap up and swing my leg over the bike, having to stand on my tiptoes to do it. I try to settle into the leather seat so my short skirt won't hike up any further than it needs too.

"Fuck," I exhale out, mainly to myself.

Jay revs his engine, and calls back to me, "Not yet babe. Save something for later," in the most smart-ass way he can.

I try to balance myself so that I can keep my hands on the seat, away from Jay. He falls into his rightful place, slightly offset behind Vince, as his Vice-President, and jerks on the breaks briefly, causing me to crash my chest into his back. So much for trying to balance myself.

"You know better... hold on," he grits through the bandana tied to cover over his mouth as he rides. I latch as tightly as I can around his waist, and he chuckles triumphantly.

"Asshole," I whispered into his ear.

He reaches his hand down and adjusts my grip lower, so it just grazes the growing bulge in his jeans.

"Baby... I love when you talk dirty."

The engines roar and throttles opened as we take off in a uniformed pattern out of the gates of the Slayer's compound and away from my new admirer, "Crotch."

I'm gonna kind of miss the bastard.

CHAPTER TWO

We ride down the highway and through downtown Chisholm. It's nearing noon and folks are setting out to lunch. Children watch in awe as the bikers speed through, some women look on in lust, and men follow the bikes in envy. Mostly though, everyone looks on in respect at the MC that keeps their town safe, and if nothing else, at least an interesting place to live. We stop at the intersection at the four corners in the heart of town, and Jay nods over to Vince. Vince raises his chin in recognition and drives on with the rest of the brothers in pursuit. Jay turns us onto North Street and heads away from the rest of the guys, into the residential part of town.

After a few quick turns we finally pull into the drive of Jay's little cape-style yellow house. He cuts the engine and sits, waiting for me to dismount first so that he can follow.

"Well?....," he gives out in frustration.

I swing my leg over, nearly toppling down to the ground trying to get my footing with my platform wedges. Jay reaches out instantly and grabs hold of my arm to steady me as he swings off his bike gracefully. He looks down at my shoes, slowly up my bare legs, and then the oversized Kingsmen tee. I hand him back his helmet, awkwardly aware of my state of half dress.

"What? I was at a Bachelorette party... what was I supposed to wear? A fucking parka?"

Jay grunts and grabs his helmet, placing the strap over the bike's handlebar, "I'm very aware of where you were last night Lil's. Now get in the damn house," He spits out with mild disgust.

"I didn't ask you for your help, Jay..."

He reaches out and gently touches my chin, moving it slightly so he can get a better look at the bruise forming on my cheek.

"Yeah... looks like you were handling everything just fine, sweetheart. In the house, now."

Amid my mild protests, Jay places his hand on my lower back and guides, well, more like gently pushes me up the walk to the front door. He slides his keys out into the lock and pushes through the door with me just behind.

He drops his keys into the bowl on the side table next to the door and kicks off his boots, setting them next to the bottom landing of the staircase. He takes off his leather cut and drapes it over the staircase railing before disappearing further into the house, toward the kitchen.

I look around, taking stock of my surroundings. Not much has changed in the last two years. The living room is set up the same with a newer, larger TV on the wall opposite the couch that we spent countless hours on... watching movies, fooling around, and falling asleep.

I step forward, searching down the hallway toward the open doors. The master bedroom door is ajar and I can just make out the corner of the bed where Jay and I made love for the first time. The bed where I lost my virginity to my man. And, it's also the bed where Jay has fucked countless women since, no doubt.

"LIL'S! What the fuck are you doin'? Waiting for the mailman? Get in here already" Jay calls out from the kitchen.

I slip out of my wedges, instantly loosing the four extra inches of height they provided. I scoot them over next to Jay's boots and glide further into the house. I used to love the feeling of my bare feet on these worn wooden floors. Once upon a time it felt like home. I would always wake up earlier than Jay and make my way to the kitchen to start the coffeepot, tiptoeing down that hall quiet as could be not to disturb him. The smell of brewing caffeine would always wake him and lure him out of bed where he would find me in only his club t-shirt making us breakfast. Here I was, barefoot, wearing his t-shirt and walking my way into the kitchen. DeJa Vu is a bitch.

I enter the cozy kitchen to find Jay has set out some sandwich fixin's and chips. He's talking into his cell phone, barely looking up at me as I pull up a stool to the breakfast bar and sit down, either avoiding me, or engrossed in his conversation.

"Yeah... she's right here. Bring over the things she'll need later." Pause. No clues as to whom he's talking to. "Ma... give me a break, OK... I said later. I'll text you."

Bingo! He was talking to Jean. His mom. My second mom growing up. Is she coming here to see me?

"Yeah. I'll tell her. Love you too. Bye."

Jay slides his phone into his pocket and hands me a turkey sandwich, barely looking up at me as I take it from him.

"Ma says hi. She'll be here later to check in on you. Bring you some things." He stares at my legs. "Some decent clothes at least. Text her the things you'll need-- any girlie stuff, you know."

I start to add on some tomato and mayo to my sandwich, completely starved. I haven't eaten since yesterday.

"Thanks... but I have a change of clothes in my car to head home in. I just need a lift to the bar to pick it up and I'll be on my way."

Jay opens the fridge, pulling out a beer and a bottled water. He keeps the beer for himself, and sits down across from me, nursing it slowly. "Yeah... about that. Change of plans Lil's. You are home."

I nearly choke on my sandwich and reach for the bottle of water to clear my throat.

"What the hell are you talking about Jay? Chisolm hasn't been my home for a very long time...."

"What the fuck do you *think* I'm talking about Lil's? You think there are no consequences for last night? You think you can just sneak into town, dressed as a whore I might add, beat the ever-loving shit out of Shade's Ol' lady, and then take off? What the fuck goes through that pretty little head of yours sometimes?"

He was standing now, pissed off and roaring down at me.

Not one to be intimidated, I push up out of my chair and stand as tall as I can. All five-feet, three-inches of me. Not much, I know, but it's what I have to work with.

"First of all, I didn't *sneak* into town. Just because I don't alert the fucking media as to my social calendar doesn't mean I'm sneaking in. Second of all, it was a FUCKING BACHELORETTE PARTY!!! This is how you dress for that. Thirdly, I didn't know she was Shade's or anybody else's Ol' lady for the record. She wasn't wearing a rag. She started shit with me first, I just finished it. We both know the bitch had it coming to her. It was long overdue." I swear I think I see his nostrils flaring.

He slams his beer down on the counter, with a loud echo. I'm surprised the bottle didn't break.

"Well she *is* his Ol' lady. And now she's in the E.R., Lil's. She needs emergency surgery. They're flying in a goddamned plastic surgeon, for Christ's sake!!!"

"The bitch needed a nose job anyway....," I try to joke, settle the tone down a little bit.

Jay reaches over to me and grabs hold of my arms, "I SWEAR!!! Do you not get it? If you had been anybody else, you'd be on your knees right now in their clubhouse being passed around for all of them to take a turn. You'd be paying this debt off on your back, princess."

I swallow hard. I know what could have happened. But the fact the this man is going to try to get off as my knight in shining armor right now is starting to piss me off. I shake loose of his grip, and shoot back.

"What's really got you worked up Jay? The fact that I came back here and didn't have the *decency* to schedule a reunion with you, or the fact that I messed up your pretty little whore?"

He looks blindsided, stunned almost. Didn't last long though. He's got the reflexes of a fucking cat. He walks towards me, causing me to step backwards trying to maintain some space.

"What the fuck did you say to me?"

I crash into the empty wall behind me, but Jay keeps on coming my way. "You heard me. Your whore. Tell me, how long did you wait, hmmm? A day? A full

32

week before you plowed your way through any available pussy you could find?"

Jay is right on top of me now. A full ten-inches taller and a hell of a lot bigger than me.

"*You* left me, remember baby? Who and when I fuck is none of your goddamned business after that!"

"Oh really? Well what about *before*, then? Is that any of my business? I saw her you asshole! I saw her leaving your room at the clubhouse. And you paid her you son of a bitch! A goddamned whore! I guess free pussy at home wasn't enough for you, hmm?" I spit ou,t trying to hold my ground against his towering form.

He furrows his brow and shakes his head. "What the fuck are you talking about Lil's? Baby, I've never had to pay for pussy. Never will either. You saw nothing... you're full of shit. You ran baby for your own fucking reasons. Don't try to pin it on me."

Furious, I push my weight against him trying to gain some space.

"I'm full of shit? The day before I left, I saw Shannon, the chick from the tattoo parlor leaving your room at the clubhouse. You were pulling your pants back up you jackass, and you had no shirt on. You paid her a wad of cash and kissed her while saying '*Thank you Darlin'*'.... Don't you dare say I'm full of shit. It's etched in my fucking memory like a fucking scar!"

Jay starts to laugh at me while backing away.

"Holy shit. *That's* why you left? That's why you ripped my heart out? You left in the middle of the fucking night! Like a fucking coward! You left me, you left your pops, and Tiny... Your ma!!! Everyone who loves you! All because of what you *THINK* you saw! Did it ever occur to you to ask me? To trust me? To have a little faith in me? I promised I would never fuck around on you. I swore it. You didn't even have the fucking decency to give me the benefit of the doubt!"

The buckling sound breaks my trance and I shoot my eyes down to where he's taking his belt off and unbuttoning his jeans. I step behind the counter looking for some bit of protection. What the hell is he doing?

"I'll show you what you think you saw baby girl...."

"Jay, don't..," I plead to him.

His eyes are stone cold. My Jay is gone, I have no idea who this is. His jeans slide down followed by his boxers. I back into the corner, preparing myself to fight him off with everything I have. I look down at his growing erection. He lifts his shirt to expose the flesh right above his pubic bone. There are black letters showing with a swirling design around them.

"LOOK!!" he bellows. "Look at what you think you saw! She gave me a tattoo. A fucking tat! I had her make a house call to the clubhouse so I wouldn't have to have my dick flyin' around for everyone to see in the middle of fucking tattoo parlor! I paid her for the TATTOO! Not for a piece of her ass!"

34

I look at the beautiful words emblazoned on Jay's inner hip, just below where his underwear band would be. The words *My Lil' One* are written out in cursive with a vine of thorns and roses around it. I gasp at the Tat, looking up at Jay. His eyes are still full of rage.

What the fuck had I done? I look back down at the artwork and swallow hard as my eyes shift over a few inches to his beautiful dick. It's huge, growing firmer by the minute. He is as mad as I've ever seen him, but the fury is also doing other things to his body. He pulls his pants up around his hips and leaves them there, not bothering to button them closed.

Moving towards me, he starts again, this time his voice has an eerie calm to it.

"Let me tell you how this is gonna work. You went after an Ol' lady. Not just any Ol' lady, but the bitch of the leader of the *one* club that wants to take us out. The only thing that saved your ass was the fact that one Ol' lady can't be touched for going after another Ol' lady in self defense."

I try to register what Jay is saying to me, grateful that he isn't yelling. "But-- I'm not an Ol' lady....."

His face contorts into a grin.

"The hell you aren't. You're mine. You said the words yourself. I claimed you then and there. You may have never gone through with getting the tat or wearing my rag because your pops made me promise to wait until you were older but that don't change shit. You

35

were my Ol' lady. And you left. So this is how it's going down baby girl. I fucking stepped up and threw down to get you out of the shit you got yourself into. I saved your ass from becoming a human dumpster for those assholes and saved the club from having to go to war to retaliate for your ass. It cost me a pretty penny, too. Don't think you come cheap, baby 'cause you sure don't. Cost me a hundred grand to Shade to pay off the Docs and meds for his Ol' lady, plus a bit for pain and suffering. You owe me. And I intend to collect every last penny."

Jay's words hit like cannon balls. One after another.

"I-- I don't have that kind of money." I feel the need to state the obvious. I'm finishing my third year of college. No way my tips from the measly bartending job I have are going to cover a tab like this.

He looks down over me once, and then again, tightening is lips.

"I'm not looking for your money, baby. You'll pay it off in trade. You swore to be my girl, my Ol' lady. You tried to bail on that. Well, that don't fuckin' work for me anymore. As long as you have my protection, they can't touch you. As long as I'm kept happy and content I may feel obliged to offer you that protection. Remember, I'm your patch-holder princess. You're my property. Always have been, always will be. You're gonna be my Ol' lady in every way, and do it with a smile on your face and a thank-you after I'm done. I was everything you needed me to be and it wasn't enough for you. So I'm not going to treat you with kid gloves this time. You're a grown woman, enough to walk out on your man and break your word. Then you're old enough to deal with the consequences of your actions. You did this. That hot little temper of yours got the best of you, and you thought you could just storm through and nothing would ever happen. Maybe next time you'll think before you fly off the handle without knowing the facts. Could save you a hell of a lot of trouble in life, babe."

I stand stunned, shell shocked, and unable to move. But, he isn't done yet.

"You're a big girl now Lil's. You make your own decision. I'm not forcing you to do shit. I'm simply telling you how its gonna be if you choose to stay. You can walk out that door same as you walked in. You don't want to be my Ol 'lady then go... go be free and I hope they don't catch up with you right away. We took a vote on this, club's on board. You leave here, you leave me, and you start a war. No way are they gonna stand around and let those fuckin' bastards do what they planned on doin' to you without retaliating. So now you know everything involved. Give me your answer."

Time stands still. It simply pauses. I think about my brother, my pop, my uncles, and everyone who loves me. Everyone who I'd abandoned two years ago and yet still stood up for me today. I think of what might happen to them if I make another selfish decision. I think of Jay, *my* Jay who tried his best to be everything I needed him to be. The boy who promised me things, and turns out never broke his word. I think of the man in front of me now. The man I'd hurt and abandoned because of my own insecurities and how he still risked it all for me.

"I'll stay... I'll be yours."

"OK, then." Jay speaks very slowly. I'm not quite sure he expected the answer I gave. "Finish up your sandwich and then take a shower. I have some calls to make."

He walks past me and leaves me standing in the middle of the kitchen. Something deep down inside me feels different. Not exactly broken, but not like before. I feel shame.

******

After what seems like a long time reflecting about how I had gotten where I am, I clean up the mess in the kitchen and head toward the bathroom to shower the stink of bar-room brawl off of me. Hopefully the lingering scents of embarrassment, fear, and shock will wash away, too. As I pass the open basement door, I take a peek down, but not enough to be seen.

The music is turned way up and I hear the clashing of weights from below. Jay has a full-size gym down there, part of his man cave. As long as I've known him, he's always blown off steam by lifting weights. It explains why the man is built the way he is. He's got more muscles than a goddamned professional wrestler. I was probably the motivation behind most of them.

I enter the bedroom we once shared. The place where we had our most private moments. The place where he held me as I cried when my grandma died, the place where we laughed until it hurt and he made me call out his name in passion.

I run my fingers along the dresser that was once mine, the oiled wood smooth under my fingertips. Opening the top drawer, I'm not sure what to expect. I rummage through some of my old underwear and pajamas. He hasn't emptied my drawers. They are exactly as I had left them. My hand feels something cold and hard at the bottom. I pull it out and stare at the picture frame. It's my prom picture. Jay and I looked so happy. So in love, so untouched by shit.

I remember the faculty nearly died when we showed up. I had turned eighteen just weeks before, and so legally they couldn't bar us from attending despite our age difference. That was also the night I gave him my virginity. He was so gentle and so loving. He made me feel like I was the only girl in the world. I reach around for any other pictures hidden away in the depths. I find one of us on his bike, and one standing in front of this house the day Jay closed on the mortgage.

I was still living at home with Pops, but Jay always told me he bought the house for me. As soon I was older and finished with college, Pop's said he would give us his blessing for me to move in, with the unspoken understanding that it would be done the right way. I would wear his patch and even his ring if he asked.

So many memories flood over me. Memories that I had pushed deep down below those of the tattoo girl and what I was sure was something it turns out it wasn't. I put all of the picture frames back on top of the dresser. I strip down, throwing my clothes in a pile on the floor, letting my hair loose from its clip and make my way into the bathroom to take a long shower.

Jay had the bathroom redone shortly after he moved in. It has a large standup shower with a built in seat, and we each have our own shower head. Knowing how much I liked to take baths, he found an old claw foot soaking tub at an estate sale. He and Tiny hauled the thing in themselves, nearly breaking the door in the process.

I turn the shower water up hot and get in, drowning my problems in lather. Hearing the bathroom door open behind me, I turn to see. The steam is rising as a barrier, hiding his shape until he opens the shower door and steps in.

He's all sweaty from his weights, and glistening. His muscles bulge from their recent strain. I look over him, comparing what I find to what I remember. There are a few more tattoos than I recall. They're all so beautiful. Jay has a thing for intricate, almost gothic body art. Not just your usual skulls, guns, and thorns that adorned most bikers.

His tats all have meaning, all were well planned out, and I was by his side when he got many of them. I bring myself to lower my gaze to the tattoo near his hip. My tattoo.

My Lil' One. It was quickly dwarfed by his growing penis. Jay must have seen my attention peak as he walks over to me.

He is close enough to press his full length against mine. The heat from the water now pales in comparison to that from his own body. He grazes his mouth on my shoulders, my throat as he grabs my ass, and pushes me even closer into him. His dick is now pressed into my belly, dropping low, and grazing the entrance between my legs.

He squeezes my ass and then smacks it, leaving a vibrating sting behind. I gasp for air mainly in shock. He's never spanked me before. As I whimper out in surprise, he plunges his mouth into mine, assaulting my lips, sparring with my tongue. I feel my arms go limp. His hands kneading my back cheeks are the only things holding me upright.

"Mmm. Baby, I'm going to take you just like this, right in here. Turn around." I look to him in confusion.

He briefly kisses me deep again before tearing away and letting loose a low guttural growl.

"I said turn around." He smacks my ass again, harder, and in the same spot as before.

I obey him and turn around with my back facing him. He kisses between my shoulder blades, nipping at my neck, before he lightly and carefully pushes my arms forward to brace myself against the tile wall.

"Baby... you look so fuckin' hot right now. I've dreamt of taking you like this. Standing still, just for me. Waiting for me to give it to you."

Turning my neck around, I want to try and see his gorgeous eyes, his chiseled face as he turns me on like this. Jay blocks me with his body, placing my hands back up on the wall as if I were about to be strip-searched, or frisked.

"Stay put baby. You move before I tell you to, and I'll have to think of a punishment...."

He pushes me further and further past any limits I thought I had. I want this man to touch me, to fill me. He continues to kiss my neck and I can feel his hands moving up and down behind me, stroking his length, pressing it against my ass cheeks and up and down the cleft between.

"Is this what you want baby. Hmm? You want me to give this to you like I used to? Like you used to beg me to?"

I'm about to explode listening to his voice, feeling him so close to me. "Jay- I... umm...."

He uses his legs to spread mine further apart, rubbing his dick up and down my heat as he teases me, applying pressure into the most sensitive areas. I can feel the tip tracing around my opening, sliding around in my slickness.

"Baby. You're so wet for me. You want it bad...."

Jay's right. I do want it bad. My head is spinning. It's been so long since I had been with a man. And it was *never* like this. Even with Jay, it was never quite like this. This is hotter.

"Wait! Jay. I'm not on anything! Please, wait...."

I give him reason to pause. He entwines his fingers in a few of my long waves of hair and twists slightly, pulling my head back toward him and his mouth.

"I fuck you where I want and when I want, baby... you're mine. Maybe I'll make you want it so bad you'll beg for it first." He lets go of my hair and pulls my ass out further to him, elongating my back out like a stretched cat.

Dropping to his knees, he plunges his face into me, kissing and licking me from front to back as I moan louder, and louder, thrashing my head back. From down below I can hear him moaning into me ,taking pleasure in how he makes me react. Slipping his hand down, he slowly slides his long finger into me, deep until it has no further left to give.

"God baby, you're are so damn tight. We're gonna have to work this out a little bit before you're ready for me, hmm?"

My breathing has since turned to panting, unable to gasp enough air into my lungs. Jay continues entering me, trying to widen me by moving his finger in circles, stretching me. His fingertips make their way to my nub and gently press, tug, and flick as his finger-thrusts grow faster, and stronger.

I feel an explosion growing deep in me, where Jay is reaching inside. My muscles tense and tighten around him, pulsating with the engorging of all my sensitive tissues.

"Baby... you're so close. I can feel it, I can taste it. Are you ready to come for me baby?"

His tongue is assaulting my opening, twirling around where he is exploring with his thrusting finger.

"Yes, yes. Jay, I need to-Please. Don't... stop...."

My words trigger Jay to release his mouth, while using his arm to spread me even further apart, and in one precious moment he slides two fingers in, using his mouth to latch onto my front apex sucking the life out of me and into him.

"NOW! Baby come for me now."

"JAY!" I explode into convulsions, with everything I have escaping me. Jay slows his finger-thrusting, and releases his mouth from my nub while I settle into the aftershocks of my orgasm. My legs shake slightly as I gain my bearings. That was the most powerful eruption I 've ever had.

He stands behind, and collects me around into his arms, picking up my fallen chin

"Baby, that was amazing. You are so beautiful..." He kisses me sweetly and tenderly as I recover. The seconds pass, growing into minutes as he kisses me deep, tasting of my juices. The scent of my need for him turns me on. I break our kiss and hang my head low, steadying my breathing. He supports my body weight against him and rubs my lower back, my hips.

"Easy baby. Shh... let it ride."

After regaining my composure, I sheepishly raise by head to this sexy man. Slightly embarrassed, I can feel my cheeks flush. He chuckles lightly and kisses me tenderly on the lips.

"Jay. That was... amazing."

He smiles at me and slaps my ass one more time, lighter than before. I rest my forehead against his chin and sigh with contentment. Maybe this isn't the worst fucking day of my life after all?

CHAPTER THREE

Jean stops by shortly after we towel ourselves dry. She barges through the front door dropping several shopping bags on the floor by her feet.

"LILS! Where the hell are ya?" She calls out into the main rooms of the house.

Tucking a towel around myself securely, I reached her in the main hall as she wanders around searching for me. Running into her arms, I nestle into her comfort and finally let myself release the stress and fear built inside from last night.

"Ma." I had called Jean that since before I can remember, as she was closer to me than my own mother. "I'm so sorry... I was so stupid."

Jean soothes me by making calming sounds and smoothing my wet hair. There is a small crack in her voice as she finally addresses me, confident that my emotional state has settled some.

"Sweetheart... you're safe now. You're home where you belong." She pulls back from me, holding my body at arms length to inspect. Taking in the bruised cheek and the circles under my eyes, she's assessing the extent of my condition. "You look like shit Lil's. You need sleep and food, and family. You've been gone way to long baby girl."

I notice her voice harden with the last few words. This woman had practically raised me, caring for me when my own parents fell short. After mom and pop split, things kind of changed at home. Jean stepped up and took me under her wing, treating me like the daughter she never had.

I can see the pain in her eyes as she searches into mine, searching to find the little girl she once loved so much. My name even came from Jean. My own mother had named me Julia after my pops mom, but the first time Jean saw me, she started calling me "Lil' one".

It shortened over the years to Lil's, and most knew me be no other name. I had abandoned this woman, just as I had left Jay behind. Crushing pressure starts to build in my chest as she looks into me.

Guilt.

Blinking back any trace of sadness, Jean perks up and forces a smile. "Well, what's done is done. You're home now, no use fussing over shit you can't change. I brought you some new clothes to get you by until your things get here. You need anything else not in here, you tell Jay or me... my boy will take good care of you while you're here" she states matter of factly. Raising her chin, she calls out behind me, amplifying her words to the footsteps coming toward us.

"WON'T HE?"

It isn't so much a question as it's a warning to Jay's sudden appearance. Jay is a badass, but his mama still knows how to keep him in check. He had managed to towel most of his chin length hair dry, the rest hanging slightly dampened and loose around his ears. Clean jeans had been put on, and he fumbles with a folded black t-shirt as he walks past us, his bare chest rippling with large muscled and colored artwork.

"Yeah ma, she's in good hands. Thanks for bringing this stuff by." He pecks his mom's cheek while pushing his arms through the sleeves of the shirt. "Help Lil's get settled and then make sure she catches some sleep. I'll be back late tonight. Any problems, you call my cell. Two prospects are keeping an eye outside. You scream like a fuckin' banshee if you need them, otherwise they'll leave you both to your girl stuff." He manages to get all this out while lacing up his boots.

"Wait," I interject, feeling as I should at least have some input as to what I am and am not going to be doing for the rest of the day- even though his orders are pretty much on par with what I am set on doing with my afternoon. "Where are you going? I'm just supposed to stay here while you go out? Maybe I have things to do?"

Jay stands up tall, passing his leather cut over his shoulders. He pecks Jean once more on the cheek and then steps closer to me.

"Maybe now you don't? You step out of this house while I'm gone, consider it an end to our agreement. I told you to stay here with ma, you stay here with ma. Don't ask me where I'm going. It's club business. If I wanted you to know, I would have told you. Now..." he trails his fingers across the top of my towel. "Cute as this is, I don't think it would be practical to wear on the back of my bike. So get your clothes taken care of with Ma, and get some fuckin' sleep."

He is terse and stern, nothing like the sweet Jay that I had just been ravaged by in the shower. I hate being told what to do, and he very fucking well knows it. I can tell he's getting off on his newfound leverage over me.

He winks his eye at me and smirks, waiting for my usual smart-ass reply. Now, I have more than a few ready and waiting to fly off my tongue... but I hold it. I'm not in a position to piss him off any more than I already have.

Satisfied with my apparent show of obedience, he smiles and pats me on the ass mockingly as he turns to head out, "Good girl...."

The next couple of hours are filled with updates, and gossip from Jean. I feel like I'm being given an abridged summary of all that I've missed while I was gone. We unpack my new clothes and straighten a few drawers for my things. Every once in a while, Jean will just hug me and tell me again how glad she is that I'm home.

I learn that Jay has been very busy while I was gone. He's lived, breathed, and slept for the club. He makes more runs than any other member, and was busy proving himself over and over to all of them. It isn't easy being Vince's son, and he's had to more than make up for it.

When he was voted in as V.P. last year, he made damned well sure that everyone felt he had earned it on his own merit- not his genetics. Because he spent so much time on runs or at the clubhouse, Jean helps to take care of the house for him. She helps with the laundry, the cleaning, and the shopping. Jay is her only child and she's a great mom to him. I've always been secretly jealous of the bond they share. Not as a girlfriend jealous of her influence over her son, but as a daughter with no mom of her own to care for me the same.

That was probably why I was so drawn to Jean when I was a kid. She oozed motherly affection and unconditional love. Don't get me wrong. If she caught you doing something you weren't supposed to be, I can guarantee you wouldn't be doing it a second time. She comes down like a ton of bricks when she has to.

It's nice to feel this motherly love again, unaware of how much I had truly been missing it. When we have exhausted all topics of conversation and hugged more than enough times to make up for the lack of them during my absence, I find that I can barely keep my eyes open as she lulls me to sleep with her soothing voice.

****

The deep vibrations of a motorcycle engine cause me to throw my eyes open wide. How long had I been asleep? I lay curled up in Jay's bed, groggy from being jolted from a deep sleep. Straining my neck off the pillow, I can see the bright neon block-numbers of the alarm clock on the bedside table. 12:18.

The living room lights flash on down the hallway. I can hear Jay and his mom talking in hushed voices, the sound of keys clinking together and finally the front door closing. The bedroom illuminates with artificial yellow light as Jean's car headlights flash through the windows before disappearing. It's amazing how sensitive your hearing can be heightened when you're laying in the dark, waiting for someone.

There are thuds of his boots dropping onto the wood floor, the clanking of the fridge door opening and closing quickly and then footsteps approaching.

I clamp my eyes shut, and try to regulate my breathing as much as I can, to appear even and deep. There are the soft sounds of fabric dropping next to the bed one after another, before the mattress finally sinks down next to me. Jay reaches out and pulls me back to his bare chest, nuzzling into my hair.

"I know you're not sleeping baby... but you sure are cute when you pretend to be." His hands slide under my t-shirt and graze over my stomach, rubbing and massaging as they roam upward.

My bra proves to be a poor barrier as his hands slip under and into it, cupping my breasts and kneading them as his hips follow suit against my backside, his growing member pulsing slightly into me. My body betrays me, buckling under the strain of pretense as I try to swallow my moans of pleasure.

In a sense of victory, Jay nips my earlobe before suckling lightly on it, "Mm... there's my girl."

His left hand plunges down between my legs and past the thin protection of my panties. Gliding his fingers through my lady lips, he strokes me back and forth while burrowing his boxer covered dick into the small of my back from behind.

"Time to wake up sleeping beauty and welcome me home, hmm?"

My teeth clench onto the nearby pillowcase and I grip for dear life as Jay's fingers play me expertly. He kneads my boob while tugging at it and rolling my taught nipple between his fingertips. Down below, he slides deeper down while stroking, entering his fingers into my opening while pressing his palm firmly onto my clit. The friction causing my already swollen tissues to throb in need.

I manage to call out through my gritted teeth. "Jay...mmm."

"NO!" Jay pulls me from the safety of my pillow to face him while flat on my back. "You call me baby when I'm fucking you."

My eyes meet his as lust clouds over and darkens his baby blue eyes. His onslaught to my lower half is unrelenting. There's so much wetness that his fingers are gliding effortlessly into me and then out to cover my nub before pushing in again. They plunge deeper and hook around towards my front, clambering to push into the secret spot Jay knows all so well.

He finds it, and I can sense the knot of pressure building, building, and then exploding as my toes curl and by neck arches up, leaving me to scream out, "God! Oh my God!"

His fingers pause, allowing my contracting walls to settle before withdrawing them. Raising his drenched hand up, he traces my quivering mouth with his pointer finger, covering me with my own moistness before licking my lips with the tip of his tongue.

"You taste so good baby girl," his tongue punches through my slightly parted lips and thrusts in my mouth, digging deep. He pulls back just enough to let his words escape.

"Get on your hands and knees."

I barely register the full weight of the order, before he is helping me up and tugging at my last remaining clothes, adding them to his own pile. He pushes my shoulders down and settles in behind me, kissing the small of my back, trailing warmth over my skin. My moans are unrestrained, hitching every time his dick grazes my opening.

Jay reaches around and slides a pillow under me while pressing me further down with his body weight until my rear is tilted up perfectly for him. He sits straight up, abandoning his kisses and presses himself against me. I can feel his dick twitch slightly when it makes impact against my leg.

Using his knee, he widens the space between my thighs by pushing my legs further apart. I scream pleasure deep into my pillow, awaiting what's to happen next.

"This was always your favorite, wasn't it baby? Me behind you, deeper and deeper into you, until you can't take it anymore," Jay's hands now grip my hips, gaining their footing for what's to come.

"You have such a beautiful ass, baby... I've always wanted you to give me your ass..."

I'm dripping down my leg and onto the sheets, my desire and my need overflowing from within. Jay's fingertips massage into my skin, with his thumb trailing its own way to cover the opening to my anus. I clench together as he starts to massage small circles into that delicate skin, applying a growing amount of pressure.

We had never done this before, I'm not sure if I'm able to let him, although his thumb is giving me intense longing to try.

"Mmm, baby. This is mine. One day soon you're going to beg me to give it to you here. But for now...," he

55

slides his cock right over the opening to my pussy, "I want to hear you scream out how deep you want it."

My hands clench into fists trying to hold in my need. The tip of his dick swirls in my wetness, lubing itself. The nerve endings in my folds are on high alert, waiting to feel the pleasure I so desperately want. I want him deep in me, pushing his way to my next explosion.

I call out to him, "Deep, baby. I need it deep." Breathlessly, I wait.

Mmm! He plunges deep into me with one thrust, bottoming out. He holds himself still while I cry out in pleasure as he fills the deepest part of me with his throbbing manhood. Ever so slowly, he starts to withdraw his length from me, hitting every delectable nerve along the way out. I can feel the sweat start to prickle the top layer of skin of my back. When at last just the head is inside of me, he grips my hips strong, and, WHAM!, pushes himself right back into me.

I cry out as I come around his shaft. My body shudders and convulses as my orgasm takes over, leaving me floating, hovering near the edge of myself. Jay massages my hips and then my thighs as I quiet down from my immense outburst. His fingertips swirl over the indented area right above the cleft of my ass cheeks.

"Right here-- right here is where I want you to get my ink," he begins to rock his length in and out of me as he plays with the patch of skin, now covered in gooseflesh from my now heightened nerve endings. "Right here where I can see it every time I make you come, deep inside."

His thrusting becomes methodical, increasing in both speed and depth. Tension is building inside of me again. The rising pressure of my growing arousal no doubt clenches on Jay as he pushes himself into me, again and again.

I lift my head back over my shoulder to see him in all his glory, pushing and pumping, delivering to me what I need. He smiles at me mischievously and growls as his neck stretches back. I need more. I use my body weight to push back into him as he meets me with his next thrust.

His eyes shoot open at my actions and he breaks into a huge grin. I didn't think it was possible for him to add any more strength behind his maneuvering, but he musters up some hidden reserve of power and pushes me past every barrier there is, into the strongest orgasm of my life. Pulling my arms back together, causing me to stand tall on my bended knees, he presses his mouth into mine collecting my orgasm screams into his kiss as we come at the same time, filling me with his seed.

We support each other with our bodies, aware that the other will collapse if we move. His dick starts to settle and return to size as he slowly withdraws himself, causing me to unconsciously hiss at the sensation. I'm beyond raw, and that last bit of friction is gloriously painful in its own right. I fall back into the mattress as Jay stumbles to the bathroom, where he rinses his battered member off. Crawling back to bed, he pulls me close to him with one arm, while pulling the comforter to cover us with the other.

Face to face, we stare into each other, with many unspoken words between us. He kisses my forehead for what seems like forever, wrapping me in his arms as I purr contentedly into his chest. He chuckles and squeezes me tight.

"Baby, that was mind blowing... but I don't think you're going to be able to walk tomorrow."

Maybe not, but it was definitely worth it.

CHAPTER FOUR

SUNDAY

The bacon sizzling in the pan in front of me pops as a small amount of grease splatters out toward me. I jump back, narrowly avoiding direct contact with the hot projectile.

"Crap," I mumble, as I turn off the flame and look down at my arms to make sure I haven't been splattered.

"You know there *is* a splash guard for that pan," Jay walks through the kitchen, making his way next to me.

Turning the tap to cold in the large farmers sink near by, he takes hold of my arm and runs it under the cool running water.

"It's not much, I think you'll live." He smirks as I stick my tongue out at him. "Mmm. I have plans for that tongue. But, first... feed me woman." He turns off the faucet, dries off my forearm, and then kisses the small, red area starting to form.

"All better."

Jay is one of the most ruggedly handsome guys I have ever seen, *even* while fully clothed in his jeans and leather. But, now, with him standing in front of me in nothing but his drawstring sleep pants tied low on his hips and his tan, chiseled chest beckoning to me, I am certain he is the finest male specimen alive.

I glance down to check his waistband to see any hint of the now infamous tattoo. Nothing. His pants are low enough for me to trace the 'V' shaped notch his muscles make near his groin, and see the bluish line of a vein reaching to his dick, but there is absolutely no sign of the tat. It's hidden, a secret, only for me to see. Well, maybe at first it was for only my eyes, but life took a turn where I'm sure countless bitches had their face right in it, staring, wondering what it meant.

I giggle, thinking of those poor girls bobbing their heads up and down staring at what was essentially my mark on him. I take in the scrumptious view as he turns away toward the coffee pot and pours himself a large cup.

"Something funny, baby?" he drawls in his sleepy morning voice as he slides over in the direction of the breakfast nook.

The front view might be fantastic but the back view is simply out of this world! His broad shoulders are like pillars on either side of him. Muscles flex ever-so-slightly as his arms move with his gait. The deep cleft trailing his spine is well cut and firm, covered by the large back tattoo that mirrors the patch on his leather cut.

The word 'Kingsmen' arches across his lower shoulders in bold, gothic letters, with a coat of arms and sword emblazoned dead center over his rib cage. Underneath the detailed artwork is the charter name, Chisolm, arching upward, just skimming the narrow part of his waist. That tattoo always makes me drip for him. Even now I can feel the liquid pool down low, ready to escape my opening.

I cross my legs and stand tall, squirming just a little as the stinging sets in. I'm raw, chaffed and swollen from last night, and the slight acidity of my liquid is not the most comfortable feeling filling into those places. Jay sits and takes a long sip of his morning drink while scrutinizing me, as I stand trying to balance myself.

"Is it that bad? Did I hurt you?"

I smile to him, "I'll be fine. Nothing that hasn't happened before." Before I can even finish my words, I realize just how they must sound to him. His eyes narrow and turn hard.

"Is that so?" he hisses.

I uncross my legs and fumbled over the cupboard, turning my reddening cheeks away from him.

"You should know, you were always the one doing it to me," I explain as I withdraw a plate and fill it with scrambled eggs and bacon from the pan before setting it in front of him. I can see his shoulders relax and lower, accepting my words for what they are... the truth. No other guy even came close to making my body feel the way Jay always could.

He picks up his fork and stabs in to the eggs. "Good... give you something to remind yourself of me while I'm gone."

I add some bacon to my own plate and sit across from him, "You're leaving? When?" I fiddle with my food, pretending not to be overly-interested in his plans.

Jay sips on his coffee while eyeing me.

"Don't try to miss me too much. Leaving in a couple of hours to make a run to Virginia. Couple of stops along the way. Nothing too crazy. I'll be gone at least ten days."

He starts to bite into his bacon, "Give you time to settle in, get your shit set up with school. Plenty of time to recover from last night before I get back," he smirks at me. A jolt surges straight down to my groin. Ouch. I need to try to stop doing that.

"About that," I let out. "I tried to tell you in the shower. I'm not on anything. We didn't use anything last night, Jay. I thought you understood what I meant?" I drop my fork down onto my plate with a small clinking sound, and search for his explanation.

"Um, hmm. I remember..." he takes another bite of his bacon. "It was one time Lil's... I don't think we have anything to worry about. But, if it makes you feel better, go to the Doc and get some birth control pills. Dewey's Ol' lady just got the shot. Maybe you can look into that. You're too forgetful for pills, anyway." He chews slowly, watching his plate.

I sit back in my chair and fold my arms across my chest, crushing my boobs. One of the biggest problems that big-chested girls have is not being able to cross their arms comfortably.

"I've never forgotten to take my pills. In all the time we were sleeping together I've never forgotten, asshole. Not once." I scowl back at him, pissed that he would even have the nerve to insinuate that I was irresponsible when it came to protection.

Apparently, my fears resonate with him as he rests his elbows on the table and leans forward to discuss the situation, actually engaging himself in the conversation.

"Why the fuck aren't you on anything anyway, Lil's? You like playing with fire up in that little college town of yours?"

Dumbfounded, I huff and grind my teeth together at his douchbag accusation.

"Not that I owe you a fucking explanation, but I don't *need* to be on anything. I haven't *been* with anyone in months. But even if I was on something, you can still pass other shit around, asshole. How do I know you're clean?"

Jay doesn't seem to like the spotlight on his own sexual activity. He clears his throat deep, "I'm clean baby... other than you, before and now, I wrap my shit up tight."

I roll my eyes at him in the most obvious way I can manage.

63

"Listen Lil's. You go get on something and I promise to use a condom until we're in the clear, OK?" He cocks his eyebrow at me waiting for me to agree.

I bite the inside of my cheek, contemplating. "Fine. I'll go to my doctor in River Rapids tomorrow when I go back to take my last final exam." I hold my breath. Let's see if he takes the bait.

"We have Doctors here, you know. We don't live in a motherfucking third-world country, Lil's," he shoots back, drawing his imaginary line in the sand.

I would need to play this very carefully, I know Jay well enough to know that once he puts his foot down, it isn't easy to get him to back down. I have one last final to take, in my Abnormal Psychology class. It's worth 30% of my final grade. If I bail on it, I will walk away with a 'C' in the class. I've busted my ass far too hard for a damn 'C'.

I push my crossed arms slightly to further plump-up my boobs. At this point, a little eye candy can only help my cause. My voice drops a couple of decibels.

"Jay, I need my things. Not new things to replace them, but *my* things. I need to take my final, give my boss an explanation face to face before just walking out on him, and take care of my lease. While I'm there, I'll stop in to see my Doctor and say goodbye to my girlfriends."

Jay is barely mulling over my valid points, so I feel the need to up the anty.

"If I'm going to come back home, I need to finalize everything up at school so I'm in good standing to transfer to a school around here. You're not even going to be here, so this is the perfect time for me to get shit squared away. This way when you get home, I'll already be back and everything will be taken care off. It's a no brainer."

I should really think about switching my major from psychology to pre-law, so I can at least get some more use out of my debate skills. I can see him struggling to stay firm with his plan.

I purse my lips tautly, waiting. I don't have to wait too long.

"I would think that behaving yourself at a bachelorette party would also be a no brainer." Crap! "But, fine. You wanna go back for a couple days and take care of your shit, then do it. You have two days max. You take Sunny with you, and I'm sending two prospects to clear out your apartment, and keep an eye on you two."

Leaping out of my chair, I run to him and fling my arms around his neck, settling-in on his lap. It isn't often that I used to be able to persuade this man to see my way on things when he had his mind set. This is definitely a victory.

"OK! I'll call Sunny and set it up. It'll be great, give us girls a chance to really get to know each other. I'll be back before you know it."

I'm practically giddy. I was so afraid that I wouldn't have a chance to say goodbye to my friends before leaving River Rapids. I mean, by the time I get back to school, if I was able to, they might not all be there.

Jay unlatches my hands from around his neck and holds them between us.

"Lil's. I'm serious. You keep a low profile and stay out of trouble. You don't go anywhere without a prospect and you check in with me. I call you and you don't answer, there's shit when you get home. You and Sunny take my truck and the boys will follow on their bikes. You let them do all of the lifting and moving. Get your records from school and your Doctor. No detours, no sidetracking."

I kiss his cheek and nod profusely at all of his requirements, they aren't unreasonable.

"Um hmm. I promise. There and back. I should go get ready and call Sunny," I go to leave the table as Jay holds on, clasping tighter around my hands, anchoring me to him.

"Are you forgetting something?" he asks, the mischief barely concealed in his voice.

No way in hell am I about to thank anyone for giving me their "permission" to go pack up my place. Apparently that isn't what he meant.

"Your man is leaving on a run for a week and you don't want to give him a proper send off?" His breaths are deep, stretching his chest as he inhales.

I wiggle my ass into his groin, enjoying the small amount of torture I can use to fight back with.

"Mmm," I kiss him deep, tasting the mocha, deep-roast lingering on his warm breath. "Doctor first baby."

He growls slightly into me, "Not necessarily....."

Grabbing my ass, he digs my hips deeper into him. My eyes perk up in curiosity. He puts his arms behind his head and leans back.

"Suck me hard, baby girl".

Jay has the most beautiful penis I've ever seen. It isn't like I had many to compare it to, but his blew every last one of them away. The shaft is long and thick, tilting up toward the end. There is a small notch right under the head that I've always used as a landmark when going down on him. It's one of the most sensitive areas, and I know just the right way to press my tongue into it to make him lose himself. The head is the softest patch of skin I have ever felt and I used to love to run it over my lips. It feels like kissing a piece of satin. The vein stalking its way down the trunk always throbs under my palms as I hold him tight, moving his skin with me as I stroke him. I can never fit his entire length in my mouth, but know just how to give attention to the rest of his dick while I attempt to anyway.

THEN

The first time I had ever gone down on Jay, I had no idea what I was doing. We were in the basement of his parent's house, watching a scary movie late one night. It was a weekend, so Butch would always let me stay out later. We hadn't been dating long, maybe four months or so, and the butterflies were definitely still there. I had become slightly more comfortable touching him, and I knew it drove him wild when I did.

We laid on his couch, kissing and petting heavily. He always paid extra attention to my boobs. I've been blessed with a great rack, and he loved to show his appreciation. My hands had recently started to explore under his pants and I found that it was no longer intimidating to hold him. He had showed me how to touch him and caress him in a way that always seemed to make him whimper in tortured pain after I had been tending to him long enough.

That night, we had been following our usual pattern of touching and groping when suddenly he started to moan and shift himself, not seeming to be able to get comfortable. I thought I was doing something wrong, so I told him I was sorry.

"Baby, you're not doing anything wrong. It just feels so good. I need to come.... I can't wait much longer" He unbuckled his belt to give my hand a bit more room.

Emboldened by his need for me, I looked dead-set into his eyes and told him, "Tell me how to make you come."

He tensed, eyeing me, gauging my level of preparedness for what he was about to ask.

"Touch me like you do, and kiss me there, like your licking an ice cream cone."

His face showed no sign of embarrassment or shame in asking me to tend to him like this. It was only full of need. If he was confident in it, then I was sure that I could be confident in doing it to him. I swallowed hard. I knew what a blow job was, I had heard about it, talked with my friends about it, and even seen it in the random porn magazines that Tiny would leave littered around his bedroom when I would quickly enter to place his laundry on his bed. I could do this. He wanted me to, and more importantly, I wanted to do this for him.

Looking back, I must have been slightly clumsy with just the sheer newness of it all. Jay caressed my hair and my neck as he was panting, moaning.

"Baby, that's it, just like that."

I had managed to figure out a rhythm to my stroking that made it easier to slide his dick into my mouth without having to readjust my grip. When I needed to breathe more air in, I would pull him out completely, and swirl the tip around my lips until I was fortified enough to bring him in again. He seemed to fucking love it when I did that.

I was really getting the hang of it when his shaft started to pulse a little faster. "Baby--baby. I'm gonna come. Let go... It's gonna come out now."

He strained and pulled himself out of my mouth, pumping himself while his eyelids closed shut and his body spasmed. His hand glistened with wetness and his shirt was now moist from the outpouring splashes. He dropped his head back.

"Fuck! That was incredible," he whispered.

Sitting there between his legs, I had no idea what to do next. Was it over? He was barely moving now. Was he hurt?

Not knowing what to do, I reached over and grabbed some extra napkins from next to the empty pizza box from earlier. I dabbed at and pressed his dick and hand trying to sop up some of the mess. It was slippery, and I couldn't seem to get it all up. Jay reached his arms through his shirt, pulling it off.

"Shit baby, you don't have to do that. Let me," he used his crumpled shirt to clean himself off before throwing it on the floor away from us. He pulled me up onto the couch besides him, and hung his limp arms around me. He kissed his lips against mine and then rested them on my forehead.

I needed to know if I had done it right. "Jay--was it... OK?"

"Lil's, you have no idea how fucking *'OK'* that was. You didn't even swallow and it was still hands down the best ever."

I backed my head away an inch and pitched my voice into a question.

70

"Wait, you mean I can swallow it?"

Jay chuckled and kissed my forehead again.

NOW

The dick in my hands is just as I remember it. Each square inch is memorized in my mind. I know how it feels, how it tastes. I push the last bit of cotton down past his hips, and down his leg. He manages to get the rest of it off by using his other foot to peel it past his heel. I spread his knees slowly, using my fingernails to lightly trail up his inner thighs, opening themselves to me.

His penis stands fully erect, bouncing from the recent move to freedom from inside his sweats. I look at it admiringly, twitching the corner of my mouth up in a mild smirk.

"Hmm. Baby, I don't know. I might not remember how...."

Jay hitches out a laugh, "Hah! Yeah right. Baby, you were a fucking *expert*, but I can always give you a fresher course if you need it."

I glare at him smartly. I stretch my back forward, practically on all fours, careful not to touch any part of him while making my way to his center. Using only the tip of my nose, I ran it up from the very base of his sack slowly to the tip of his very erect head. Lingering over his pink apex, I started to blow a cool stream of air directly into him. I can hear him hiss from above. I lift my gaze to his face without moving my head, as it's perfectly aligned for what I'm about to do. I raise my eyebrow, arching it high in a slightly evil way.

As slow as I can, I open my mouth wide and curl my lips loosely over the edges of my teeth. His eyes are watching me intently, studying my moves without blinking. I lower myself millimeter by millimeter, taking his dick into my warm mouth more slowly than I even think possible. His eyes widen further the more I take his cock in. As I reach the bottom of his throbbing shaft, I close my eyes dreamily, and tilt my head just the tiniest bit to the side. I extend my tongue as softly as I can to cradle the underside of his length with, and then forcefully move myself up his erection just a bit faster than when I took him in.

"FUCK!" Jay calls out as I assault his favorite body part, reaching the head as my tongue swirls over and around the tip in my mouth.

I can feel Jay's hips buck just a bit as I suckle on him gently, roaming my warm breath over his opening. I feel the beginning of his pre-cum start to seep out onto my tongue. His familiar musk floods my senses, giving me the driving force to step up my game.

I clamp my lips down around him, sealing him in tight and then suck in as hard as I can. Using my hands to balance myself, I look once more at Jay's anguished face. Because it's never really a bad time to be bit of a bitch, I wink at him before I send myself crashing down again, causing him to moan out loudly and breathlessly.

Every skill that Jay had taught me was put to use. Each little move deliberate and unrelenting as I touch, pull, push and suck my way into the deepest depths of Jay's need. He squirms and whimpers and begs me as I unleash myself fully to my task.

Jay had known me as an innocent girl and helped me blossom to a passionate lover, desperate to please her man. But this part of me was new to him, unfamiliar to him. This is a woman aching to please him because it pleases me more in doing it. Every fulfilling twinge he felt, I feel exponentially greater. His need is my need, and I would see to it that it was completely satisfied or die trying. I impress myself with my own stamina, considering how long it had been since I had done this.

Jay bites his lip and calls out to me, "Baby, I'm gonna come-"

His eyes fly open and watch me continue the job at hand. His brow furrows and purses itself as he tries to pull his hips back away from me. I haven't always finished to the end with Jay. He never made me feel like I had to accept his flow into my mouth. It depends on the moment.

"Baby! I'm gonna come!"

Well that is the point, isn't it? He shakes with each mini-eruption that flows from his manhood and trickles into my waiting warmth. He throws his hands deep into

73

my chestnut waves and massages my scalp as I set to task, licking his juices clean off of him. When I'm finished, he bends down to kiss my lips deeply, breathing heavily. I stand up into his kiss and then pull my mouth to his ear.

"Have a safe trip baby," I whisper huskily.

Now that was a goddamned send off.

CHAPTER FIVE

Tiny answers the phone on the second ring, breathless and panting.

"Yeah., what's up bro?"

"Umm... no. It's Lil's. Catch you at a bad time? Sunny there?" I can hear rustling on his end, as I picture him jumping to his feet to match the sounds passing through the phone.

"Sis... you OK? Where's Jay?" he blurts out.

I realize that I've called him from Jay's home phone, but really, what's all the excitement here?

"Tiny, I'm fine. Jay's here. I need to ask Sunny a favor. She around?"

My brother holds his breath before answering, "Yeah... she's right under me. Can this wait a bit Lil's? We're kind of in the middle of saying goodbye."

Ew. What the fuck? No way should Tiny be sharing this information with me. I picture Sunny giggling below him.

"You are a goddamned animal, Tiny! I cannot believe you just said that to your own *sister*. Tell Sunny to call me back when you're done molesting her," I hang up the phone and stomp into the bathroom to shower, trying to shake the image from my head. I can hear Jay laughing from the kitchen.

After showering and dressing, I make my way out to the living room where Jay is hunched over the coffee table. The strong scent of artificial banana hits me as soon as I near him. My stomach constricts and a lump draws in my throat. The locking and clicking sounds confirm what I already know to be true. Jay's cleaning his handgun. The gun cleaner and cotton balls spread over a few pieces of newspaper in front of him.

I have always hated when he cleans his gun in front of me. I know he carries, hell all the brothers do, but I don't need a fucking "in my face" reminder of it. When I was a young kid before my folks split, ma would always make my dad maintain his pieces out in the garage. The intense banana smell of the cleaning fluid made her dizzy. I nervously sit down in the armchair across from him.

"Goin' fishing?" I say as sarcastically as I can.

Without looking up from his project, he cocks his head to the side, checking the barrel before releasing it with a loud snapping sound as it closes.

"Something like that baby," he slides the clip of bullets into the handle and slams it into the heal of his hand to ensure it's secure before standing and tucking it into his waistband, pulling his t-shirt over the area.

Shrugging his shoulders at my obvious disdain, he smiles. "Never too safe, baby doll. Sunny called back when you were in the shower. She had to rearrange a few things and clear it by Tiny, but she can go to River

Rapids with you. I told her you'd pick her up in a few hours. Tiny gave her the same speech I gave you, so we're all on the same page. No need for miscommunication on either end. Two days. That's it."

He scurries to crumple the dirtied newspaper and toss it in the wastebasket.

"Prospects are out front. Give them a heads-up when you're ready to head out. The truck's all cleaned out and gassed up," he pauses and looks directly while pointing his finger at me for emphasis. "And Lil's... *DO NOT* change my radio stations to your damn girlie music."

I giggle. It took him almost a week to figure out how to change them back the last time I had done it. Served him right for spending an un-godly amount of money on that involved of a sound system. I can see that Jay had showered and packed a small duffel bag waiting by the door.

"Come here," he uses his eyes to motion from me to in front of where he stands.

Jay reaches into his back pocket and pulls out a thick letter-sized envelope. As soon as I'm in range, he pulls me into him and places the envelope between us, tapping it against my chest.

"This is for your little trip. There's enough in there to pay out your lease and take care of anything else you girls need up there. You need more, you tell the tall one, Blue, and he'll take care of it."

When I don't take the envelope from him, he pulls out the bra shelf of my tank and slips it in. I begin to refuse the cash when he clips my chin between his fingers and holds it firm. "DO NOT give me any shit. You got your way, quit while you're ahead Lil's."

I sigh and resign myself to let him think I'm going to take his money. Jay's other hand snakes behind me and cups my ass deep, almost straight through between my legs and holds firm.

"Mmm... gonna miss that sweet pussy of yours."

I clamp my thighs together holding his hands in a vice.

Jay laughs, "If I wasn't gonna be late for church, I'd bend you over and smack your ass for being such a little cock tease."

Standing up onto my toes, I plant the sweetest little kiss on his lips, and then turn to whisper seductively near his ear. "Don't get yourself all hot and bothered baby. You've got a long ride ahead of you and I wouldn't want you to squirm the whole way thinking about little ol' me...."

I squeal as he slaps my ass and then rubs it rough.

Jay slams his mouth onto mine and groans down into my throat. He pulls away in a quick jerk, grabs his duffle and stalks off in a huff.

Before he closes the door behind him, he calls out. "Two days," leaving me standing in the middle of the empty living room with a wad of cash between my tits and the need to change my panties.

******

Jay's truck roars to life as I throw my overnight bag into the back seat and fiddle with the buttons on the armrest to bring my dangling feet closer to the pedals. The air conditioning blasts out at full speed helping to cool the warm leather interior as the navigation screen illuminates.

Driving a truck this large will take some adjusting, as I'm used to driving my little Toyota Prius. The oversized pickup truck is new enough to still have a lingering plastic scent in the double cab, and other than a half-rolled pack of lifesavers in the change bin it's kept immaculate. Jay never does anything small. Not his bike, cars or least of all his temper. I need to strain to see over the wheel comfortably.

I slowly roll out of the driveway and check oncoming traffic before turning out. The two prospects assigned to me for the trip are already geared to fall in line behind me. I've known Tommy, or T.J. as the boys called him, from high school. He was a couple of years behind me, and I had homeroom with his older sister, Tara. The taller one, Jay had called him 'Blue', seems nice enough but must be relatively new on the scene because I've never met him before.

My driving must be as awkward as I fear, because the bikers stay far enough behind me to benefit from whatever advanced warning my brake lights can provide. I head over to the other side of town, where Tiny and Sunny live. I like Sunny very much but have only gotten to see her a couple of times when Tiny brought her with him to visit me at school.

They've been together now for a little over a year. She's a few years older than me and had moved to town from Atlanta when she had inherited some old house from an uncle that passed on. After hooking up with my brother, he moved her into his place and they rented out her house to a sweet old couple.

My brother is nicknamed Tiny because he is the exact opposite. He was a linebacker in high school and weighs at least two hundred and fifty pounds of stocky muscle. He inherited pop's thick, dark brown hair along with me, and keeps a year long tan. Sunny is the polar image of him.

Unlike my brother's road name, she *actually is* tiny. She can't be more than five foot three and is as fair skinned as they come. Real peaches and cream type of complexion. Her light blonde hair is always perfectly cut and styled, with dark lowlights the last time I had seen. Sunny is a great hairdresser, and my brother had set her up with her own shop here in town.

I glance up at myself in the rearview mirror and shake out my own head to give it some volume, thinking that maybe she could spruce me up a little when we get back from our trip. I'm a pretty low maintenance kind of gal, but it might be fun to let her experiment a little. I pull up in front of Tiny's house and tap the horn a bit. I don't want to be rude, but I think it's safer this way rather than to try and park in the driveway only to have to back out again later.

T.J. and Blue pull in behind me and dismount. Sunny comes strolling out of the garage, teetering in her high heel sandals, while pulling her wheeled Luis Vuitton carryall behind. She waves her hand behind her, pointing her keys and the garage door closes automatically. The prospects meet her toward the apron of the driveway and relieve her of her luggage, with T.J. heading toward the back cab to place it in the bed of the truck. Blue opens the passenger side door for Sunny, and helps her make the climb in, closing the door behind her.

Sunny and I hug and squeal together, ready to start our adventure, when a set of knuckles rapping on her window draws our attention. Sunny lowers the window with her control switches and we both lean over to Blue. He's tall enough to be on eye level with us, even in our raised seats.

"All righty ladies, we head straight to your apartment from here. You need to stop for anything, you send me a text and we'll pull over. Jay says to keep it under 60 or it might be too much for you to handle

81

the brakes. We good?" he askes us both, before nodding and tapping the car door as he turns to his bike.

"All right. Let's roll."

Sunny raises her window and we both keep a stoic face until we're sure Blue is well out of earshot before we burst out laughing. I put my best macho-man impression on and lower my voice to match his.

I throw on my sunglasses. "All righty ladies... we good? Let's roll."

Sunny bursts out into hysterics. "That was soo good. Don't let him hear you do that though, I hear he's a real tight ass."

My curiosity was peaked. "He seems nice enough I guess. Say... why do they call him Blue? He's got *brown* eyes."

Sunny's hysterics return and she needs to gasp several times before she can muster up a response.

"Well, I hear he gets off on girls giving him blue balls. Some twisted, sadistic shit."

I stare straight ahead, stunned at Sunny's explanation. All righty then. I doubt I'll ever be able to look at Blue the same again. I join Sunny in her laughing and we head north out of town.

****

Chisolm isn't much of a town compared to most, and it doesn't take us long at all to leave its borders behind. I take the main interstate that will lead us directly into River Rapids. My apartment building isn't far from campus, with most of its tenants being students like myself. It's no Taj Mahal, but it's clean and it's cheap. It came fully furnished, and the Super is always pretty good about fixing and repairing things. I have about seven months left on my yearly lease, and pray that the landlord would let me break it without too much hassle. He should have no problem finding another tenant, especially with the kids staying around to take summer classes and all.

I've been able to save up a decent amount over the last two years. I received a scholarship for daughters of veterans, that covered all of my tuition and even some of my other expenses. I was damn lucky to find it, too. Otherwise, I would be drowning in student loans like most of my friends will be one day. My paychecks and tips from tending bar at the brewery downtown covered my measly rent and car insurance. I had to cut some corners here and there but I live pretty comfortably for a college junior.

Knowing Jay as well as I do, I'm fairly confident that he won't take a penny from me, no matter how hard I try to pay my own way. If I take the thirty five hundred dollars out of my savings account to cover my lease, I should still be left with around six hundred or so and I can pick up a job in Chisolm to help me build up my cash reserves again. I should probably stop by the bank on my way into town to withdraw the cash before they close. I have Sunny text Blue that we need to stop at the Bank of America branch on Main Street.

Our little entourage pulls in the front lot of the bank. "Hang out here for a minute, I'll be right back."

Sunny hands me my purse and I scoot out of the Truck. Blue lifts his sunglasses and gives me a quizzical look. I hold out my hand to him gesturing 'one minute' and file into the brick building.

I complete a deposit slip at the main counter for thirty seven hundred dollars to give myself just a little extra cash to tide me over for a while. Waiting on line, I fumble through my bag for my wallet, to prepare for the teller.

My license isn't in its usual slot. Hmm.I search every other built-in pocket and notice that my debit card is missing too. I haven't had to use either since before the whole bachelorette party incident, and start to panic that they had been stolen or left behind, when I find a piece of folded paper.

LIL'S- USE THE MONEY I GAVE YOU

Fuck. That son of a bitch set me up. The next available teller is calling out to me. I give him a shy look, apologizing.

"I'm sorry, I forgot something," I storm out of the bank, crumpling the withdrawal slip as I walk.

Blue perks up at my hasty exit, and I call out to him, "If you talk to Jay before I do, you tell him what an asshole he is for me!"

Blue holds up his hands as if he had nothing to do with whatever I'm upset about. I slam the truck door behind me and throw my purse down next to me.

"Everything alright, Lil's?" Sunny looks worried. I turn the engine on and bite on my lip.

"Perfect. Everything's fucking *perfect*."

It takes us no more than ten minutes to reach my building. Parking in my usual spot proves tricky with an automobile triple the size of what usually parks here, but I manage. T.J. and Blue carry our bags up to my third floor apartment. They also carry their sleeping rolls.

I set up Sunny in my bedroom with me. Blue and T.J. will have to crash in the living room. One lucky bastard will get the couch. I'll let them work that out between themselves.

We all agreed on Italian for dinner and T.J. sets out to pick up our phoned-in order. Blue is a man of few words, but manages to discuss a plan of attack for packing up the apartment. With none of the furniture being mine, as the apartment came fully furnished, only my clothes, computer, TV, and cooking stuff will need to be packed. Sunny volunteers to pack up my personal things.

T.J. returns with dinner, beer, cardboard boxes and packing tape, allowing us to finally set down to eat, as he gives me an update on Tara. She's married to some electrician, and they live just outside of town with their one and a half year old daughter. She's about five months pregnant with their second child. T.J. is the dutiful uncle and shares pics on his phone of the cute little girl playing with her dolls.

Wow. Tara is my age and she *already* has kids? That's just crazy. I mean that would be like me... FUCK. In all the excitement of the trip I had forgotten that I need to stop in to see Dr. Foster tomorrow, and get a prescription and a checkup. I suddenly feel very uneasy about the beer I'm holding, setting it down and excusing myself to turn in early to get a good night's sleep before my final exam tomorrow.

I wash up and brush my teeth before changing into some yoga pants and a t-shirt. Sunny hangs out with the prospects watching some alien movie, and so I shut my bedroom door to keep out some of the noise. I grab my phone and check my messages, where there's a text from Jay.

JAY: SO APPARENTLY I'M AN ASSHOLE? MISS YOUR SWEET ASS.

Jerk. Not only does he force me to take his money, but he's trying to make light of it. I type a reply that I know will piss him off.

ME: HEY BABY... I'M BACK IN TOWN. YOU BUSY LATER? OOPS. SORRY. WRONG PERSON.

I settle into my blankets with a cheshire grin, and close my eyes. No sooner have I gotten comfortable do I hear the light ping of my phone. I try to ignore it, but curiosity eventually gets the better of me.

JAY: NICE TRY BABY. STILL MISSING YOUR SWEET ASS.

I'm not overly tired yet, so I might as well entertain myself for a bit. I pick up the phone.

ME: GOOD. I HOPE YOU GET HARD THINKING ABOUT IT.

JAY: OH BABY I'M HARD ALL RIGHT

ME: HOPE YOU DON'T GET A SORE WRIST

JAY: MMM BABY IM RUBBING IT OUT RIGHT NOW

ME: YOU ARE NOT!

**JAY: AM TOO... I CAN SEND A PIC TO
PROVE IT IF U WANT**

ME: PIG!

**JAY: OK... NO PIC. HOW BOUT U SEND ME
A PIC INSTEAD?**

I think about this for a minute. This might not be a bad idea. I get up to lock the door and then shimmy out of my pants and underwear. I quickly snap a picture of my lady-bits and hit send before dressing again and getting back in bed.

ME: YOU LIKE?

**JAY: GOD BABY! YOU ACTUALLY SENT ME
A PIC! FUCKIN BEAUTIFUL...
MMM I WANT IN THAT TIGHT PUSSY**

**ME: YOU EVER HOPE TO SEE IT AGAIN
THEN YOU GIVE ME MY CARDS BACK**

**JAY: ALRIGHT ALIGHT I WILL..
YOU DRIVE A HARD BARGAIN**

GETTING LATE. WHY U UP?

ME: CUZ I HAVE A CRAZY MAN TEXTING
    ME :)

JAY: OH I'LL SHOW YOU CRAZY. :)

ME: U CRASHING FOR THE NIGHT?

JAY: YUP
     WHAT TIME IS YOUR TEST
     TOMORROW?

ME: 9

JAY: GET SOME SLEEP
     NEED TO BE ON YOUR GAME
     2MORROW

ME: K
    HOW BOUT U?

JAY: IN A BIT
     STARTING OUT EARLY IN THE A.M.

ME: GETTING SLEEPY

JAY: CLOSE YOUR EYES BABY

THINK OF ME

ME: MAYBE :)

JAY: AND BABY..
THANKS FOR THE PIC

CHAPTER SIX

MONDAY

I'm one of the first people to hand in my final exam and to exit the lecture hall. It wasn't anything too crazy. A short essay, some multiple choice, and a case study. Piece of cake. I'll start checking online for the grading next week.

The student services building isn't far from my testing site in the humanities quad. It's late morning and the campus has that carefree summer break vibe to it. Frisbees being thrown across the lawn, bicycles zipping by and the occasional sunbather litter the grassy knolls between buildings. T.J. has been elected to accompany me around while I run my errands, mainly because he's more age appropriate to blend into the college crowd. It probably would have helped if he left his leather cut at my place, but it seemed like blasphemy to even suggest it.

We make small talk and joke a little about some of the freakishly dressed people passing us by. He's ruggedly cute, and doesn't yet radiate "pissed of biker bad ass" yet. Give it time, I tell myself. After all, Jay had once looked semi-innocent. I notice many of the girls checking T.J. out, some casually and others blatantly obvious. He's a nice guy... hopefully he finds himself a nice girl and doesn't get too swept up in the free club pussy hanging around back home.

I leave him chatting up one of the Delta Tri Sigma girls in the lobby of the student advisor department when I'm called in to meet with a counselor. I explain that due to family needs, I'll be moving home to Chisolm and will apply to several local colleges for the fall semester.

I have to fill out some paperwork, mainly regarding my scholarship, am handed a manila envelope with an unofficial transcript and am officially un-matriculated. The whole business takes no more than forty minutes, but when I search the lobby for T.J. he's nowhere to be found. Hmm... that's odd. I don't have his cell phone number or any other means to try and contact him.

The receptionist hadn't noticed him to help me find where he might have gone off to. However unlikely, he may have headed back to the apartment. Either way, I'm sure I'll meet up with him at some point. It'll be nice to have a little privacy for my next errand, anyway.

I catch the next express campus bus to Main Street, and head over to the River Rapid's women's health office. I had called-in earlier this morning to schedule a quick appointment with my Doctor, and the receptionist had been very nice to squeeze me in. The wait times aren't usually very long in this office, but I pick up the newest issue of *US Weekly* and prepare to get caught up on all the latest celebrity nonsense when my phone buzzes.

JAY: SO HOW DID THE TEST GO?

I didn't expect to hear from Jay until tonight. I know they don't stop too often when making a run.

ME: PRETTY GOOD
    WON'T FIND OUT 4 A WHILE

JAY: I'M SURE YOU ACED IT
    I HAPPEN TO KNOW FROM
    PERSONAL EXPERIENCE THAT
    U R A QUICK LEARNER AND AN
    EXCELLENT STUDENT

ME: OH REALLY?
    AND HOW DO YOU KNOW THAT?

JAY: I SEEM TO REMEMBER YOU
    PLAYING THE
    SCHOOL GIRL AND ME BEING THE
    TEACHER

Flashbacks of Halloween three years ago flood over me. I had dressed up as a naughty little co-ed, a la' early Britney Spears, and Jay had found a nerdy professor costume. I blush and instinctively tilt my cell so no one can read my incriminating phone screen. Jay had given me some private tutoring lessons that night, mainly on the primal mating habits of mammals and the male anatomy.

As I try to think of a witty comeback, a middle-aged woman in grey scrubs calls out to the row of chairs, "Julia? Julia Kaegan?"

I toss my magazine back onto side table and set to follow her back to the exam rooms.

ME: GOTTA GO

The exam room is very sterile looking, and smells of hand sanitizer and latex. I follow the nurse's instructions and change into the paper examining gown with the opening tied at the front and sit on the stiff exam table, waiting for the knock at the door that is soon to follow.

The knock is light, with Dr. Foster and the nurse closing the door behind them as they enter. The Doctor is beautiful, in a middle-aged academia sort of way and greets me warmly.

"Hi Julia, how's everything feeling this morning, hmm?" She glances over my chart and begins to scribble some notes in pen.

"Hi Dr. Foster, thanks for seeing me on such short notice." The doctor simply nods as I greet her, with her eyes buried in my manila file folder, so I continue. "I'm actually here for a prescription of birth control pills."

Doctor Foster clicks her pen and closes my chart, placing it on the counter, turning to me.

"I see... It's good to see young women taking responsibility for their bodies. Tell me Julia, have you been on birth control in the past? Do you know the benefits and drawbacks to the pill? There are other options available such as the patch, the Nuvaring, and even a tiny implant in the underside of the arm."

I nod, taking in all of Doctor Foster's suggestions. "I've been on the pill before. It worked well, I just didn't have a need for it so I stopped taking it about six months ago."

The doctor sits down in her rolling stool and sits before me, gloving up. "Lie down sweetie, let's check things out and get you set up with a prescription."

I recline down to hear the crinkle of the paper barrier beneath me as I shimmy down on the table and place my legs in the stirrups. I feel something cold enter me, and the pressure from the expanding of her metal instrument.

"Julia, I must tell you that although birth control pills are almost 100% effective when taken correctly they do not protect against the transmission of sexually transmitted infection. Back up birth control such as condoms should always be used to prevent those."

I am now being poked and prodded from the inside out and feel a dull soreness left over from Jay's own internal maneuvering the other day. Embarrassed, I feel the need to explain.

"You see... my boyfriend and I were wanting to use protection. But, we did have a slight unexpected accident the other night." The nurse hands her a large Q-tip looking stick and plastic vile. After a small amount of discomfort and swabbing, the vile is sealed, cotton stick tossed into the garbage pail along with the Doctor's gloves and she stands up casually.

"Julia, if there was unprotected internal ejaculation I cannot rule out a pregnancy. Any clinical signs would most likely not be detectable this early. A blood test would determine any hormonal changes indicative of early pregnancy in about a week or so."

Dr. Foster now walks around to my side and begins a breast tissue exam while continuing her well-rehearsed speech. "I can write you a prescription for birth control pills to be taken on the first day of your next period, if there is a next period. If you have any increasing symptoms such as nausea, extreme breast tenderness, or a positive pregnancy test before then, disregard the prescription and set up an appointment for your first prenatal visit. I can also give you a prescription for some pre-natal vitamins to start taking. If you are not pregnant, they won't do any harm. If you are, they can only be beneficial, especially when taken as early as possible."

Completing my exam, she jots a few more notes down in my chart and fills out two sheets of her white prescription pad.

"The chances of conceiving after one incident at this point in your cycle are not very high but it is possible. Make sure to use condoms now through the second week of your pack of pills, to avoid any other exposures while you may be fertile. Here are the scripts," she hands me the sheets of paper. "Do you have any other questions?"

I take the papers and lowered my eyes from hers, concentrating on the floral design embossed on my exam dress.

"Umm. Actually, I was wondering what my options would be to help ensure that I don't miss my next period... I mean, isn't there something I could do this early on, just in case?"

Dr. Foster sets her pad and pen down on the counter, and takes a seat on her rolling chair again.

"I see. Well, if the intercourse was the other night as you mentioned, you may still be able to take Plan B, or the morning after pill. It can be effective if taken within seventy two hours of unprotected sex to prevent implantation of a fertilized egg. If that is the route you would like to go, you can purchase it over the counter from the pharmacy when you fill your birth control prescription. As a medical professional, I cannot advocate one choice over another. It needs to be a well thought out decision. I can give you some literature on it to read through. Please call me with any concerns or questions you may have."

I nod to her. "Thank you Doctor. I'll think about it. Guess I'm good to go?" I stand up and head over towards my pile of clothes on the padded chair in the corner.

Doctor Foster and the nurse head out the door. "Have a great summer, Julia. We'll hear from you soon."

******

The local pharmacy is two doors down from the medical building. I'm relieved that not many customers are in the counter area when it's my turn to speak with the pharmacist. I drop off my prescriptions and tell the woman that I would also like to purchase the Plan B. She types some notes into her computer and tells me to return in about an hour.

Having at least sixty minutes to myself, I decide to kill some time by calling some local friends to meet up for a farewell night out. Most of them travel home for the summers anyway, but they don't yet know that I won't be back in the fall.

I pull my phone from my purse and gasp at the amount of text messages flooding my screen.

UNKNOWN: HI LILS... ITS T.J.
UR IN UR MEETING AND SOME GIRL
WANTS
TO SHOW ME AROUND A BIT WHILE
UR IN THERE.
TEXT ME WHEN U GET OUT.

Shit. So that's where T.J. went.

UNKNOWN: LILS... U STILL IN MEETING?
ITS BEEN AWHILE...

I quickly scroll through the majority of the texts.

UNKNOWN: LILS.. PLEASE GET BACK TO
ME IF I DONT HEAR FROM U IM
GONNA HAVE TO CALL JAY.. HE'S
GONNA FLIP HIS SHIT IF I
DO THAT. PLEASE PLEASE TEXT
ME!!!

I check the time stamp on the last text. It was sent two minutes ago. Fuck! What if I'm too late? I quickly send a reply text to the number on the screen.

ME: HEY T.J. DIDN'T GET TEXTS TILL
NOW

99

I have to wait barely a moment before I got a response

UNKNOWN: THANK GOD! JUST DIALING JAY.. WHERE THE FUCK R U?

ME: RAN ERRANDS. I'M AT THE DRUG STORE ON MAIN STREET WAITING ON MEDS

**UNKNOWN: STAY THERE
I'M ON MY WAY**

Hopefully I got to him in time before he called Blue or Jay. I sit down on the stone bench and take a deep breath. That was close. The last thing I need is a pissed off Jay breathing down my neck right now. Looking for a distraction from the last bit of craziness, I dial and hold the phone to my ear.

"Hey Julia! Where you been?" The call answers on the third ring.

Emily was my roommate from sophomore year, when I transferred here. She's a real sweetheart and we've become close friends.

"Em, I just got back last night... stayed a little longer than I planned on, catching up with people."

I hear a gasp on the far end of the phone, "Wait... catching up with who? You saw him didn't you!" Hmm. Let me think about how to answer this. Technically I did see him, all of him.

"It's a long story, Em. Let's meet later at the *Drunken Co-Ed* before everyone heads out. I've got a friend with me from back home, I want to show her a little bit of town before she leaves."

Emily knows everything about Jay and I. She had seen me at the rawest point fresh after I had left him to move here and start a new life. She had handed me the tissues when I was bawling my eyes out over him, talked me down from giving in and calling him, and eventually acted as my wingman when I was on the rebound. There was a short time where I was rebounding just a bit too hard and Emily had helped to give me a guy intervention before things got out of hand.

"You did! I knew you would. Eventually anyway. I want to know *everything*," Emily is a loyal friend, but she is also a sappy romantic at heart. She always plays devil's advocate when it comes to Jay. She's never met him, but had fallen in enviable lust with his picture and declared that "no man that fine should ever be walked away from" at least a few dozen times.

I smile into the phone."Emily... I'll fill you in, I promise. Meet me at the *Co-Ed* at nine. Do me a favor? Call Jessica too. She didn't answer before, and I've got a ton of crap to do."

Her deflating tone is almost as funny as her teenage-style boy frenzy.

"All right, all right. Nine. But I want details. And pictures if you have them, but lots and lots of details." We end the call just in time for me to greet the motorcycle rider pulling up to a screeching halt in front of me.

"Holy crap that was fast... be careful T.J., this place is crawling with ticket-friendly campus police that would just love to lock your ass up." I barely have time to stand to my feet before T.J. has dismounted and shaken out his helmet-confined hair.

He stands tall and I notice that he's flushed. I also notice the lipstick around his neckline and that his t-shirt is on inside out.

"Lil's why the fuck did you run off? I could have caught so much fuckin' shit from Jay over this. Thank God it was nothing. Please, please, please don't tell anyone about this. I really don't need them jumping all over my ass because I lost sight of you."

The poor guy is visibly upset. I can understand why, too. I remember when Jay and Tiny were prospecting. They had fucked up on more than one occasion and been raked over the coals for it. I know it's part of the process, and kind of a right of passage but I like T.J. and I don't want to see him fall out of the good graces of the club for something that may or may not have been my fault.

I smile, "Don't mention it. It'll be our little secret. So tell me, how was your first sorority girl? She live up to her reputation?" I joke with him. I had never seen such obvious display of post coital disarray before.

T.J. laughs. "Who said she was my FIRST sorority girl? But damn I think I like college."

I roll my eyes. He is definitely living up to the Kingsmen standard.

"I can't even." I make an over the top gagging impression. "Let me go check and see if my order is ready. I'll be back in a minute."

The Pharmacist has my little white bag ready on the shelf when it becomes my turn at the register. He scans a barcode, and I pay the man the $68.43 that he asks for, taking my sack of meds.

T.J. sees that I'm carrying a medium sized bag and begins fumbling to open the side saddle of his bike. He reaches out to take the paper package from me, as I nervously grasp on to it. He wasn't expecting such resistance, so when he pulls the bag, it tears apart and the contents spill onto the concrete beneath us.

I practically throw myself down to pick up the items before he can get to them, but damn, the boy has quick reflexes and beats me. He absentmindedly picks up the bottle of prenatal vitamins and holds them out to me with one hand while his other picks up the colored packaged that's very clearly labeled "PLAN B".

FUCK.

103

T.J. looks at the medications briefly before registering the meaning of what he holds, when his eyes shoot up to mine.

"Lil's.... "

I grab my things back from him and add a slight coldness to my voice. "If you don't want Jay to find out that you were too busy fucking a cheerleader in a short skirt to keep an eye on your mark, you'll keep your mouth shut about this, T.J."

He swallows hard and hands me back the items in question.

******

Sunny has almost everything of mine packed and labeled in cardboard boxes when we get back to the apartment. T.J. is keeping a small distance between us, undoubtedly scared form my earlier threat. But, he manages to smile genuinely at me whenever I catch his glance in passing. He's always been polite to me, but I notice a slight uptick in his chivalry over the course of the afternoon. He takes advantage of every opportunity to open a door, offer to get me a drink, open a window, close a window, or turn on the air conditioner.

At this rate, either my little secret is going to be uncovered, or he's going to get his ass beat from the guys thinking he's a little too sweet on another club member's girl. I need to talk to him and get him to turn it down ten notches before anyone notices.

Blue runs out and gets us some sandwiches from the corner store while we finish the packing. Taking our lunch outside to the porch area, we sit down and take a meal break. Sunny sets out an old blanket for us and we bask in the mid-afternoon daylight, enjoying our subs and discussing the lack of fashion sense that college girls are showing these days. Sunny, being the fashionista that she is, notices that all of my neighbors have barely combed their hair and are still wearing sweats at three in the afternoon.

Looking down at myself self-consciously, I wonder where she thinks I fit in with the girls I surround myself with. I have on dark, stretch capris and a tank top. My hair is piled high in a pony and I put on just the basic amount of makeup before slipping out to my exam this morning... a little bit of blush, some mascara and tinted lip balm. I don't want to tell Sunny that this is actually a slight step up from my usual weekday attire.

Blue sits down in the lawn chair near us, and takes a bite of his lunch.

"I know what you mean Sun, do they actually think a man is going to look twice at them like this? I mean don't get me wrong... I'd lay pipe with any one of them but doesn't mean I wanna look at them twice while I'm doing it."

We laugh. T.J. comes through the sliding doors with an arm full of his own lunch, a bag of nacho chips and three opened beers with a bottle of water. He hands Sunny her beer first, then gives his brother the next, while setting the last one down next to his own chair. Blue grabs the bag of chips as T.J. loosens his grip on it to reach over to me and hands me the bottle of water. He smiles to me as I look to him in shock. Beginning to bend down to sit, he catches himself as if he remembers something. Reaching into his pocket, he draws out a small apple and tosses it to me.

Sunny and Blue stare confusingly at the guy like he has two heads. She hardly finishes chewing what's in her mouth

"You trying to tell her she's fat, T.J. or what?"

I close my eyes as he nervously squirms to get comfortable in the cushioned chair. He takes a small sip of his beer to mask any signs of discomfort, but I can still see them.

"What? Nah. Lil's just doesn't strike me as the junk food kind of girl. Hell, she could even stand to gain a few pounds."

I need to change the topic fast, create a distraction. I swallow my sip of water.

"And look at their hair Sunny... no decent salons around here. The girls let it go until they can get home to have it taken care of. I was thinking you could take a stab at mine when we get back. You know, nothing too drastic, maybe shorter, some color... I don't know. What do you think?"

Sunny lights up, dropping her sandwich onto her plate in excitement. "I have some brand new color that I've been dying to try. We'll cut it on an angle, shorter in the back, and...."

Blue throws a chip in his open mouth and adds, "Hold on there... you might want to think about that before you do it. You're Ol' man is anything like me, he likes it longer."

Sunny and I look at each other and then back to Blue, waiting for the rest of his sentence to help make sense of his comment. He doesn't seem like the type to have a hair preference or anything, just so long as it's on a willing female.

He takes another sip of his beer and sits back a little. Noticing our attention, he acts surprised, "What? You know... reigns."

I roll my eyes just as Sunny lets out a forced sigh. "You're all pigs."

We laugh. I roll my sandwich wrapper and napkin together and sit back, resting on my arms behind me, stretching out, soaking in some vitamin D.

"Just wait until tonight. You'll see these girls turn into runway models. No use wasting perfectly good makeup and clothes on classes, you know. We'll head downtown around eight and grab some dinner before we meet up with some of my friends for a drink."

Sunny loves my suggestion, and nods enthusiastically. Blue shrugs his shoulders, "Whatever... so long as you clear it by Jay first, I don't see why not. Might as well find me a sweet piece of ass to make my trip memorable."

T.J. chimes in from his corner seat, "I don't know... It's been a long day. You know, maybe we'll call it an early night, yeah?"

Blue just tilts his chin down, staring at his friend, lowering his sunglasses just a bit to get a better look at him.

"You OK there brother? You get hit on the fucking head or something? Since when do you turn down grade A college age pussy?"

T.J. seems to realize how odd he's acting, especially in front of another club member. He straightens his shoulders and takes one last swig of his drink., "Brother, I'm just recovering from the blonde sophomore riding me like a goddamned pogo-stick while Lil's was in her meeting."

He shifts his crotch with his hand for emphasis before adding, "Need to get me some rest before I go looking for round two, you know what I mean?"

Blue looks satisfied with T.J.'s explanation and stands up, collecting the trash from his meal. He takes my handful of crumpled wrapper and nods, "You make sure Jay knows your going for a night out, and we're good to go, Lil's."

"I'd better crash a bit then, before we head out. Lil's you should probably do the same... with bein' up early today and all, yeah?" T.J. calls out as he follows Blue in the building. Sunny scrunches her forehead quizzically. Damn, this kid is about as sharp as a fucking rock. At this rate, he'll be cutting up my food for me and tucking me.

CHAPTER SEVEN

The late afternoon sunlight floods through my westward bedroom windows. Despite my lack of enthusiasm for T.J.'s veiled recommendation, I actually *am* tired. The last few days have been such a whirlwind of unexpected life changes that my mind has barely been able to keep up.

Slipping out of my sandals, I close my curtains to the daylight outside and slip under the covers for a little bit of rest. Sunny had shared the queen size bed last night, and I wasn't quite sure if she would be following my lead in catching a nap. I slide over to one side and leave her plenty of space in case she decides to come in while I'm sleeping. I fiddle with my phone and check for missed calls or voicemails. None. Disappointment flashes briefly, before my fingers mindlessly select a contact number in my directory and press on it.

The phone rings several times before it's directed to a generic voicemail prompt. Sighing, I end the call and switch to the text message screen. Emily's text messages are brought up and I add a message.

ME: DID U SPEAK TO JESS?

I yawn, and stretch out my legs.

111

**EMILY: HEY! YUP. JESS WILL B THERE
BOBBY TOO
9 PM**

Bobby is Jessica's gay best friend. I had met him one night in the ladies bathroom at a pub downtown. Jessica was crying because some guy had stood her up, and Bobby was consoling her while trying to prevent any more damage to her eye makeup. I could barely keep from laughing like a damn hyena, watching her whimper about how he could have been the love her life, while Bobby was dabbing at her eyes with a paper towel and trying to steady an eye pencil to touch up at the same time. There was some kind of analogy about not needing Mr. Right, but instead, looking for the Mr. Right Now that was going to rock her fucking world that night and she couldn't be scaring him away with raccoon eyes.

I had known Jessica from a few classes and thought it only polite to hand over my powder compact, not sure how it would be received. I was after all, eavesdropping. Bobby took it graciously and even commented on how it was just the right shade for my complexion. We spruced Jessica up and all headed back out to the bar together. Jessica found a random hookup within minutes and left Bobby and I together to spend the rest of the night buying each other rounds of shots. Every girl should have a gay guy friend. They give the best blow job tips.

My phone buzzes abruptly with an incoming call. Jay's picture from my contacts flashes on the screen. I roll over onto my side and slide the phone to my ear while accepting the call.

"Hey, baby. I didn't think you'd be able to call back for awhile."

The reception isn't fantastic but almost all of his words come through. "We just stopped to gas up and grab a bite. What's up princess?"

His voice soothes me like a lullaby as I lay here, the room darkening ever so slowly around me.

"Not much. Thought I'd check in on you guys and see how things are going. You busy?" I close my eyes and try to picture Jay in front of me, speaking to me in person rather than who knows how many miles away.

I can hear Jay exhale into to receiver, "Baby you know I could never be too busy to talk to you. Just ordering some burgers while your brother takes a leak. You OK? Sound a bit blah."

My feet are flexing and pointing, trying to rid my body of the building pressure that his voice is igniting. "I'm OK, I guess. Just a bit, I don't know... Lonely."

"I see... How lonely?" Jay's voice drops an octave and takes on a raspiness that I know means he's definitely giving me his undivided attention. "Tell me Lil's."

My legs are now slowly moving about, trying to settle into a comfortable position. "Hmmm. Well let's just say that I'm not so sore anymore... but I want to be."

Jay starts to grumble deeply. "Lil's, you're killing me. Baby I want to feel you so bad right now. When I get home I'm gonna show you how much. Can you wait till then? Keep yourself busy... get your stuff done so you can come home and get settled. That'll take your mind off it."

My hips circle in reflex to the sound of him. This is torture.

"If I have to." I lick my lips, imagining us all snuggled into his bed, making up for lost time.

Jay calls out to Tiny in the background, to tell him he needs another minute. "Baby you're giving me a hard-on, and unless your brother wants to see me take care of myself here and now I need you to talk me down."

I laugh, picturing Tiny waiting outside a bathroom door for Jay, unaware of how his best friend was rubbing one out thinking of the guy's little sister.

"Alright, alright. I'm almost finished packing. We're gonna head downtown in a little while to grab some dinner and meet up with some friends to say goodbye."

"Sounds like a fun time... any guys you need to say good bye to?" The hidden message trailing below his words isn't lost on me.

Jay is in no way homophobic, he just doesn't associate with too many people outside of the club, and last I checked the Kingsmen had no gay brothers.

"It should be fun. No guys that I know of other than Bobby, he's my gusband."

I can hear the pause on the other end. "Your *what*? Did you say *gusband*?"

"Yup, my gay husband. I can't wait to introduce him to Sunny. They have the same fashion sense. It's gonna be epic," I explain. Even bikers should be up to date with the latest terminology.

Jay laughs, "I can't wait to tell Tiny. Text me when you get home, and behave yourself. You don't have a great track record when it comes to bars lately, you know."

Oh here we go. I roll my eyes. "You send *one* measly bimbo to the E.R. and you never live it down, jeesh."

"Alright, there slugger. Just do yourself a favor and play nice. I'm already a hundred grand deep. At this rate, your gonna bleed me dry." Jay can barely keep his voice serious.

I click my tongue in mock disgust. "Hey, I thought we were bartering here, hmm? Pretty sure I paid off at least a grand the other night."

Flashbacks of Jay holding my hips firmly in front of him while filling me deep, makes me shudder. He must sense my need, as he moans briefly, "Baby you're worth every penny. Why don't you spend the next few days

115

thinking of ways to knock your down some more when I get home."

So much for trying to change the topic. "Oh, I already know how to pay it off. Already planning your homecoming. Bobby's gonna give me some tips, you know."

"Well that sounds promising. Your brother's about to eat my food, I gotta go babe. Text me when you get home, kay?"

We both remain quiet, not sure what we are waiting for the other to say. Wanting to end the awkward silence, I whisper "I will. You be safe," before ending the call.

I bring up a picture of Jay on my phone and hold it close to my heart as I close my eyes and drift into sleep, searching for a piece of him in my memory.

THEN

The cool night air brushing past me quickened as Jay squeezed on the accelerator. I had grown comfortable on the back of his bike by now, but when he sped up I instinctively held tighter to him. The sun was hanging low in the sky, adding a purple hazed backdrop to the landscape around us. I remember as a child when my dad would take off on his bike to 'clear his head' thinking it just another excuse to bolt for a while. I had

116

never truly grasped the calming effect that a long ride can have on a person.

The fresh air entering my lungs was cleansing me. The speed we were gaining underneath us was exhilarating. The crispness around us sends a little chill through me. If not for my little fitted jacket, I would be freezing, but the English leather was keeping the whipping wind from my skin.

Jay had given me the jacket a few nights before, on my eighteenth birthday. Butch had made him promise not to offer me his rag until I was finished with school... and that meant college, too. Jay had made the best of his options, and given me that jacket instead. It looked innocent enough, with its smooth grain and fitted seams. My name was embroidered on the wrist in script. However, hidden on the inside, below the neckline, were a few more words embroidered into the lining where most eyes would never fall.

JAY'S LIL ONE.

I felt so proud to wear his jacket, my man's jacket, even if it was to remain unspoken to everyone else. I rested my cheek onto Jay's shoulder and breathed in his scent. The leather of his cut was so familiar to me now. I wiggled my way up a few small inches to be as close as I possibly could, pressing myself into him. Jay moved one of his hands and rested it on my outer thigh, squeezing firmly while expertly steering our course with the other.

The steady vibrations coming from the motor lulled me into a dreamlike state, completely content. I had been Jay's girl now for a little over a year and this man had become my everything. When we were close like this, I could just block out the rest of the world and pretend that we were the only two people that mattered. Jay slowed the bike gradually as we turned off the main road and onto a gravel side street.

I raised my chin slightly under his ear, "Is this it?"

Jay had found some secret little place on one of his last runs for the MC, and I had been looking forward to this night all week. He had promised that it would take my breath away, and with each passing night I grew more anxious. I was just wrapping up my senior year of high school and things were stressful to say the least. My mom had made it very clear that she didn't have much to give me in the way of financial help for college next fall. Pops had gotten into some pretty involved assault and battery charges a couple months back and had been away serving some time. I didn't have the heart to take a dime from him, knowing that he was going to need everything he had, to pay his fines and support his household while he was away. Tiny had just bought his house across town and was doing extra runs with the MC to make ends meet.

Jay had told me not to worry about tuition. He had offered to pay the entire thing and was actually pretty pissed off when I refused. It had caused our first big blow up fight. No way could I let him, or the club, pay for school. I wasn't naive... I knew that almost everything Tiny and I had growing up from the roof over our heads to the clothes on our back came indirectly from the club. Dad wasn't the most ambitious person... he fell short more times than not when it came to child support and financial obligations. I had taken enough charity growing up that I felt the need to draw a line when it came to college.

That's why I had been ecstatic when I received notification that I had been selected to receive a full-ride scholarship to any state school I chose, from an association that provided merit-based tuition assistance to children of veterans who served during operation Desert Storm. Dad had inadvertently come through for me. Not only did it make the difference of whether or not I would be going to college, but it also gave me a legitimate reason not to take Jay's money. He did however insist that if I wasn't going to let him pay for tuition, than at least he was going to pay my living expenses while I was in school so that I wouldn't have to bust my ass working part-time and then trying to find the time to study, on top of spending time with him. My living expenses were pretty low and Jay already paid for most of them, so I didn't see the harm in agreeing. I babysat most of the kids of the club members pretty regularly, and that added enough money in my pocket where I wouldn't have to ask Jay for much.

We pulled the bike up into a clearing and parked it under a large overgrown tree. I got off first, setting my riding boots down on the sandy ground while Jay killed the engine and followed. Leaving our helmets on the bike, he pulled me close and kissed me tenderly before grabbing my hand and leading me down a path.

"Come on, there's just enough light left to really take it all in."

The path was winding, but well-worn, climbing up into a large hillside. This secret little place of his was obviously known by more than a few others. When we reached the top, I was only slightly out of breath but still managed to gasp at the view in front of us.

We were high up top of a large platform-like cliff overlooking a valley. I knew it couldn't be Chisolm that we were seeing, having driven more than an hour to get here, but whatever town this was that we were peering over was picturesquely breathtaking. The tiny little homes were methodically mapped out around the curving streets. The water tower and church steeple rise high, as if protecting this private little sanctuary.

Jay stood behind me, and I leaned back into him, resting my body against his. He wrapped his arms around me tightly, nuzzling the top of my head. I whispered my awe, "It's beautiful. It's like a perfect little picture."

"Mmm... it is. But, wait a few minutes. It gets better."

To most, his voice would sound normal, but I had learned to read the subtlety behind it during the course of our time together. I could tell when he was nervous, mad, aroused and plain old pissed off at me... plenty of practice on that last one. That night, his voice sounded like a well-veiled open nerve. It's not something I had gotten to experience often, but it was usually pretty serious when I did.

Moments passed slowly as he held me, tight and secure enough where I felt completely safe and protected. It was also tight enough against him so that I felt the growing mass between his legs.

The sky darkened around us to a maroon covering, and in an instant all of the lights in the town lit. It was amazing! The streets were mapped out in little yellow dots navigating their way around this little piece of Americana. The sun began to set slowly at first, inching its way down the horizon, before being swallowed by unseen forces below the tree line. I hitched my breathing, in awe at the divine scene taking place.

"I love you."

I turned quickly to face Jay, and stare at the beautiful mouth speaking these words to me.

"I love you Lil's. I know you know it, but I need to say it to you. I need you to hear it, to feel it, to see me saying it to you."

I tried to swallow, but my throat failed me. My mouth was drying, my heart racing. Jay had made me feel special, wanted, cared for. He even made me feel loved, but in all these months he had never said the words. He had alluded to it, beating around the bush but never told me straight out how he felt.

He held his hands up to my head, cupping it in between, eyes searching over mine. "Lils..."

"I- I love you too."

He smiled, caressing my cheek with his thumb, lowering his lips to mine, gently imploring my lips to respond. His kiss deepened and took hold of me. I felt like I was being lifted high, flying above this sleepy little town, climbing to heaven. I needed this man, wanted him for myself in this moment and always. An urgency grew between us and a passionate frenzy took hold. He guided me blindly to a tree and pressed me against it, as I moaned out to him.

He paused, grasping for words. "I need you baby... I can't wait anymore"

I gulped hard. I knew this was going to happen eventually. Jay had been as patient and understanding as he could manage with me, teaching me and sharing things with me... but I hadn't been able to give myself completely to him yet. I had been scared, afraid that I wouldn't measure up to the many before me. Hearing him say what he just said to me, though, I knew I was ready to be with him in every sense of the word.

I had been smart about what I knew was going to happen sooner or later. I had gotten myself down to the women's clinic and started birth control a few months back. I knew I didn't want Jay and I to end up like my mom and pop, unexpected young parents forced to stick it out for the sake of the kids as long as we could. I wanted better for us, for our love story to have a happy ending.

I pulled off his leather cut and tossed it gently to the side, "I need you more"

We started pulling frantically at each other's clothes in between deep, mind-crushing kisses, and deliberate touching. I began to fumble with Jay's belt as he balanced his weight on his arms pinning me to the tree.

"You sure Lil's? I mean you sure you're ready?"

I pulled his jeans down and buried my mouth in the crook of his neck kissing and licking a trail to his panting mouth. "Make love to me... please".

In one quick move he hoisted me up guiding my legs to grab on, circling around his hips. He began kneading at my breasts, milking them with his mouth. I arched my back against the warm bark, waiting for him when the moment was shattered.

Jay pulled his head back and stared, shocked, as we listened to the phone ringing from the pile of clothes on the ground. It was pain in his eyes as he wrestled with the decision.

"FUCK. Baby I'm sorry. It could be important."

He gently placed me down and reached over searching for his phone, glancing at me apologetically. Finding his cell he quickly placed it up to his ear, "Yeah, man this better be fucking good.."

I felt exposed out here in the wild, and covered myself with my tank top, waiting. Jay's eyes widened.

"Shit. Where? OK, anybody else? Where is he now? She's here with me.. I'll bring her there."

Jay slammed the phone into his pocket and called out to me.

"Get dressed... we got to head back."

I stood still, not sure of what just happened. Had I done something wrong, had he changed his mind? I began to tremble, tears starting to well behind my eyes. Jay finished dressing, then came over to me holding my shoulders.

"Baby... I need you to listen to me now, OK? Something's happened. We need to get back, get to the hospital. Tiny's been shot."

CHAPTER EIGHT

NOW

Sunny and I blast the music booming from the docking station as we prance around the bedroom, shimmying into our shoes, and putting the final touches on our outfits. She's getting a bit of a head start on my hair makeover, and I can't stop glancing at my reflection in the full-length mirror, impressed with my new look. My lack of hair savvy aside, Sunny is gracious enough to at least let me select my own clothes. I don't have much to choose from, with almost all of my things being packed, but am impressed with what I'm able to pull together.

My black leggings hug me in just the right way, adding a bit more curve where I need, and lift my butt enough for it to stand to attention. I wrap myself in a purple, sheer, chiffon camisole and pair it with a pair of stacked ankle booties. It's a bit racy, sure, but I look like a freakin' nun compared to Sunny's micro-mini dress and stripper heels. I had heard once or twice that one of the benefits to having breast implants was that you don't need to wear a bra. I wasn't necessarily sure that I believed it, but Sunny is sure putting the theory to the test. Tiny had bought them for her as a birthday present.

Blue and T.J. are waiting for us in the kitchen area, sipping on a couple of beers prepping for our night out. I'm sure it'll be considered tame compared to some of the club parties, but I have no doubt they'll hold their own. They're both freshly showered and trimmed, with just a touch of cologne. The local college girls will be dropping their panties at just the sight of them in their bad-boy leather.

"It's about damn time. You girls tryin' to starve us over here?"

I stomp my foot and make mock gorilla arms. "I am big strong man... feed me now." I taunt Blue with a lively audience egging me on. "Come on," I hook my elbow through his, and lead him through the front door.

"You can be my date tonight. Well, at least until I get ditched for the first available horny undergrad, and then I'll have to nurse my broken heart with some ice cream wondering where we went wrong...."

Blue is so much fun to tease. I know for sure that the only way I'm getting away with it is because of Jay, but I can live with that, and Blue is being a good sport about it. He does however draw the line at having me chauffeur us all downtown. Apparently, it's very unmanly to be driven around by a chick.

We park on a side-street and head to *Rodeo Rick's,* a great western-themed BBQ place complete with mechanical bull, and line dancing. We enjoy steaks and ribs, having more than a few laughs. Somewhere between Sunny's third and fourth beer, she decides that she will ride the bull. There's no way that this will end well, but Sunny will hear none of it.

She makes her way over to the padded corral in the rear of the dining room, 'borrowing' some guy's cowboy hat along the way. It's no easy task to hike herself up astride the oversized saddle that dwarfs her tiny frame.

"Lil's! Take my picture for my man. I want him to know what he's missing." She holds on tight to the center saddle horn and pins her knees to the leather.

"I put fifty on her not lasting more than two minutes," I call out to T.J.

He smirks, "I'll take that. You care to go double or nothing?"

Hmm. A hundred bucks could more than pay my way tonight without having to touch Jay's money.

"Deal. Two minutes starts now." I check the clock on my phone, and hold my breath as the cheering crowd grows. With thirty seconds to go, I start to grow nervous. T.J. just stands, smugly watching on, as Sunny is now hooting and hollering like a cowgirl.

Ten seconds. Five seconds. Shit. Two. One. Ugh. I hang my head low in defeat and hold a crisp hundred dollar bill out. T.J. snatches it gingerly from my fingertips and leans over to be heard above the crowd.

"Let's just say that Tiny brags about his ol' lady when he drinks. I never doubted her for a minute."

Does anybody grasp that Tiny is my *BROTHER*! I roll my eyes and head off to the ladies room, leaving T.J. and Blue behind to cheer Sunny on. The restaurant is starting to pack in, with it nearing eight o'clock. The drink specials will be starting soon, and college kids on a budget know just how to stretch their drinking dollars. Squeezing my way through the kids, I reach the bar and flag down a bartender.

"Cranberry and club please."

"Put that on my tab, sugar."

I turn to face the deep voice from behind, curious at who would be eavesdropping on my drink order. This was interesting.

"Hey, Gary. Long time no see." The bartender hands me my drink, and nods over to Gary, acknowledging the financial arrangement. "Thanks... but you didn't need to do that."

"I figured it would give you a reason to have to stay and hang with me for a while." He smiles. "I mean, you've been too busy to return my texts and calls lately, who knows when I'll get to see you in the flesh again. You look fantastic by the way. Different, though."

Gary had been a small blip on the radar a few months back. We had gone out on a few dates and he even invited me to spend Christmas with his family. He was sweet and charming, but the initial spark soon faded, and he didn't seem to catch on.

I sip on the tiny red straw floating in my glass, and buy myself a few extra seconds before having to explain myself.

"I know, things have been so crazy for me. Barely a second to myself with so much going on." I nod for emphasis, but I can see Gary leaning his ear in, to hear my words, with the music and the voices becoming louder around us.

"Can't hear you Julia," he touches my elbow lightly. "Let's find a quiet spot"

I look around for any sight of my group, but too many people are blocking my view. I nod to Gary and let him guide me out, before the ever-growing crowd crushes me into the bar. We settle into a corner table, and I set my drink down, with Gary pulling in close.

"So where you been, Jules?" he takes a sip of his beer before placing it next to my own glass.

Gary's cute, in a frat boy, Abercrombie and Fitch kind of way. He's a good person and I had had a great time with him, but don't see the point in wasting any more of it for either one of us. He had clearly wanted more from me than I could give. I was looking for a good time and he was there. I had tried to let him down gently and maintain some sort of friendship, but he always found some way to try and make it more, becoming more and more possessive over time.

Distance was the only way I could find to make myself clear.

In another life, who knows what would have happened between us, he really was a nice guy and I didn't see the need to play games with him.

"I'm actually glad I ran into you tonight. I can say goodbye in person, I'm leaving tomorrow to go home."

"I thought you were hanging around campus for the summer? Since when do you go home for break?"

"Not for break, Gary. For good. I'm transferring and finishing up local. There's some family stuff going on," I smile, genuinely sad to know that I probably will never see Gary again.

His eyes pin on me. "What? Why the hell would you do that?" He holds out to latch onto my arm, trying to comprehend what I was telling him, closing his fingers tight around my wrist.

"It would be in your best interest to let go of her, asshole." My eyes shoot past Gary and onto T.J., who has found us.

I jump to my feet, closing distance as quickly as I can to buffer the tenseness growing between the two men.

"T.J., this is Gary, a friend. I was just telling him that I'm moving home. You know, saying goodbye."

T.J. clenches his jaw, twitching the muscle. "Someone should teach this boy some manners. It's not *nice* to go grabbing ladies."

130

Things are escalating quickly. Strangers nearby are unconsciously moving away, forming a bubble around our little spectacle. Gary pushes back his chair, hard enough to send it tumbling behind.

"Who you calling *boy*, asshole?"

"Seems to me that I was talking to you, pretty boy."

This is not happening. I jump in between them, holding my arms outstretched to either of the men. Gary grabs hold of my arm and pulls me out of the way, hard, whipping me into a nearby table.

"Now you're gonna fuckin' bleed, frat boy," T.J. is fast to push into Gary and send him reeling, trying to catch his balance, before he starts punching. I had never seen Gary so much as yell at another guy, let alone get into a bar room brawl, but even if he had, I know that he is no match for T.J.

The club had conditioned him well and he's used to speaking with his fists, rather than his words. Gary puts in a good effort, but is no match for the strong biker coming down on him.

Blue and Sunny break through the crowd as things start to wind down. Gary is fading fast, slunched over, and losing whatever momentum he had started with.

T.J. lands one last punch in Gary's gut before he leaves him crumpled in a corner. Several bouncers have made their way to us and are pushing at T.J. to leave. It doesn't matter that they hadn't seen how the fight began, they saw how it ended. No way were they going to let someone like T.J. hang around.

We follow behind as the juiced-up bouncers toss T.J. toward the sidewalk. Blue reaches him first, patting him on the back, proud of his friend. Sunny and I stand back, tending to my arm which is now aching from the impact from Gary's push.

"You alright there, kid? Settle down... he's out cold," Blue reassures T.J.

T.J. shrugs Blue off of him, "Yeah... no thanks to you, asshole. Thanks for having my back. Nice to know you're there when I need you." T.J.'s words drip with sarcasm. "Where the fuck *were* you anyway?

No sooner are the words out, than a bouncy, red head clearly over the legal limit comes stumbling out to us, fixing in on Blue.

"Baby... where'd you go? I thought you were going to take me for a ride on your bike?"

"Fuck off, I'm busy." He spits out to the girl, who whimpers and ducks back inside. T.J. slaps him hard on the back and starts laughing.

******

We reach the *Drunken Co-ed* in record time. My arm has quieted down some, Sunny is still wearing the tan Stetson hat and the boys hold up the rear, reliving the commotion from before. I don't like the idea of Gary being knocked on his ass, but I also don't exactly like being tossed around like a rag-doll either.

Jessica notices first, as we walk into the bar and calls us over to the booth they had secured in a corner. Emily and Bobby are deep in conversation and wrap up abruptly, when I sit down next to them, and slide my way in so that Sunny can follow.

Bobby looks Blue up and down before nodding his approval. "Yep, I would move home for a piece of this deliciousness, too, Julia."

I laugh aloud, encouraged by Blue's obvious uncomfortable confusion, "This isn't him, Bobby. He's working. Sent two friends to help me move. This is Blue, and that there is T.J."

Bobby holds his hand out regally, but neither biker knows quite what to do with it. I move on with the introductions, while they figure it out. "Jessica, Emily, meet the boys."

Jessica stares at the men in front of us while Emily blushes and looks quickly at her drink. Bobby sits back and purses his lips, deep in thought before asking out, So, I hear you guys like to ride?"

Blue turns white, clearly uncomfortable. "I'm gonna go find a replacement for the girl you cost me before, bro," he calls out to T.J. before taking off.

I shake my head at Bobby. He loves to pull crap like that. He can spot a homophobe from a mile away, and loves to play games with them.

133

Sunny laughs at the entertainment, and holds her hand out to him. "I'm Sunny, and I LOVE your highlights, by the way."

And that was it. Fate had brought these two souls together, and the rest of us have turned into chopped liver, or wors- last season's clearance rack. They huddle deep into the booth, and engross themselves fully in fashion-police style conversation.

Jessica has caught the attention of a nearby waiter and flags him over. "Full round of beers please, and shots of Petron."

T.J. edges his way in on the far side, away from Bobby. Emily nervously puts down her phone and starts small talk with him. When our drinks arrive we toast each other with the small shot glasses. T.J. eyes me cautiously, as I hold it up to my unparted lips and then place it back down on the table, it's contents undisturbed. I roll my eyes at him as he smiles satisfactorily at me before concentrating on Emily.

Sunny and Bobby break their conversation long enough to include me. I explain to Bobby that I'll be leaving tomorrow and he sheds a tear. Not missing a beat, Sunny hands him her compact mirror to repair the damage to his makeup. We all laugh, Sunny not realizing that we've just come full circle.

Jessica promises to keep in touch, and to call me on a regular basis. Emily just looks lost. "But- but... we were supposed to graduate together, remember. We made plans."

My heart sinks. Emily doesn't make friends easily, due to her shyness, and I had been her first friend here. I transferred in when we were sophomores. She had gone her whole freshman year barely noticed by any of the other students.

Bobby holds out his hand to her across the table. "Don't you worry about it, girlfriend. I'm not going anywhere."

Em's eyes light up and she accepts his pledge of continuing friendship. T.J. puts his arm around her shoulders, and pulls her close."Don't sweat it baby doll. You can come and see her whenever you want. You can even stay with me, if you need to."

Em blushes and gets to know her new suitor a bit better.

Jess and I leave the two couples to their conversations and head over to the bar, "So Jules, is he worth it?"

I take a deep breath, contemplating the question. My fingers instinctively move to touch above my belly button. I smile.

"Yep... He's absolutely worth it."

CHAPTER NINE

TUESDAY

The ride back to Chisholm is a smooth one. I drop Sunny off at Tiny's house, and then head home with Blue and T.J. in tow. Pulling up in front of the house, I notice my Prius parked in the front, giving me no other option than to park in the driveway.

The boys help me bring my things in, stacking most of the boxes in a spare bedroom before heading off, leaving Jean and I to unpack them. We make good time, all things considered, even accounting for our dinner break. Jean whipped up some of her famous fried chicken before we set her up in the bedroom next to Jay's, and we each turn in for the night.

Vince is on the road with Jay and Tiny, so Jean and I are keeping each other company. I start running the bath water and add some lavender scented bath oil to the tub as it fills. Lighting a few candles, I dim the lights, and sink into the oversized tub, grateful to finally have a few moments to myself. I touch the control pad on the nearby wall, and gentle music streams through the hidden wall speakers.

Closing my eyes, I breathe deeply, exhaling fully using the techniques I learned in yoga class to release stress. The music swarms around me, surrounding me in the sweeping melodies. I've always loved music, and find that it helps me through some of the most difficult periods of my life.

THEN

The waiting room outside the ICU was filled to standing room only. Every Kingsman within fifty miles was there to show support. Many of the wives and Ol' ladies were jostling about, making phone calls to organize things, and make arrangements.

It wasn't often that tragedy struck the club, but when it did, I knew how they pulled together. I was usually on the other side of things, though. Jay held my hand as he led me through the sliding doors into the chaos.

Jean rushed toward us as I started to break down, Jay rubbing my back as I sobbed in his mother's arms. She soothed me and offered me sweet words while Vince came over and took me from his wife's embrace.

I managed to quiet myself long enough to ask, "What happened?"

Vince held me tigh. "We're still not sure, sweetie. We were riding alongside a caravan of shipping trucks, offering protection. Some bikes came out of nowhere, trying to highjack the delivery. They fired some shots before we could chase them off. Tiny was hit in the chest. He just got out of surgery. Your ma's in there with him now."

I lifted my head, sniffling and nodding. Beth, Clink's Ol' lady handed me a tissue. "Can- can I see him?"

"Of course you can... follow me sweetheart." Jean led me to the nurse's station, and arranged for me to see Tiny.

No more than two visitors were allowed in a time. My mom was sitting in a side chair, holding Tiny's limp hand. There were wires and cords coming out of him in so many places. Monitor screens beeped and buzzed around us, and a respirator pump inflated itself and then collapsed before repeating.

"Mom..." my voice cracked watching the broken woman before me stare blankly.

"They shot my boy." She stated coldly, matter-of-factly.

I pulled up a chair next to her. My mother was barely forty-two years old. She was once a beautiful, stunning woman with the gleam of life in her eyes. She had become bitter, hardened, and worn, from a life that sometimes treated her unfairly- but mostly was just disappointing to her.

"Out there..." she pointed toward the door. "They shot my boy."

"Mom... they're going to catch the guys that did this," I tried to reassure her.

My mom collapsed her head down to Tiny's fingers. "It don't matter... they'll be another one lined up. Don't you get it, little girl?" She started to get loud. "This is what happens when you ride with those people," she spat in disgust, pointing her chin sharply in the direction of door.

I sighed. My mother had always spoken badly of the club. She blamed it for everything that has gone wrong in her life, from a husband that always put her second and eventually was lured away when things got tough, to a woman that nurtured her children better than their own mother could.

"This is what is waiting for you, baby girl. Take a good, hard, look." She was cold, detached. "Do you know how many times I sat by your daddy's hospital bed? And what do I have to show for it? A man who screwed around on me and took off every chance he got to live out some childhood fantasy. Left me with two hungry kids to feed, and now I have to relive it all over with you two."

My legs went numb. She was unleashing her pain and her hurt at me like bullets, each one tearing into my own flesh.

"Tiny's gonna follow the same dark path as Butch did. This is where it's landed him, and *you*," she was screaming under her breath, spittle snaking out with each hard syllable.

"You think that man of yours is gonna be any different? He's gonna chase every little skirt he can, while you're at home fixing his dinner. And then you'll even get to sit here in this chair, watching these machines, hoping and praying that he survives and finally wakes up to live his life right. And all the while those animals will be out there, just waiting for him to be useful to them again- for him to come running back to them. And he will.... he always will. Because he will *always* chose them."

I lifted myself up gingerly out of my chair, and shuffled out of the room, bracing myself against the railings in the hallway. I made my way down the hall towards the waiting room. There were security guards blocking the entrance to the ICU, holding back the men I had always relied on to protect me. But no one was there to protect me from the deadly words that struck my soul. My vision became blurred and my eyelids weighed heavy against me. I lost all sound around me as the ground came rushing to console me. The last sight I had, was of Jay breaking through the barricade and running towards me.

Many hours later, I woke to find myself cradled in Jay's arms as he gently rocked me back and forth, kissing my forehead. The room was dark, but I could tell that we were in his bed. My eyes were sore and swollen, raw. There was light music playing nearby. I closed my eyes and let the sweet sounds carry me away.

******

NOW

FRIDAY

The deep aroma of brewing coffee greets me as I start to stir. I take stock of my surroundings, finding myself in Jay's bed. The scent of dark-roast beckoning me to the glorious caffeine that awaits.

Jean is fully dressed in her dark-rinse jeans and tucked-in button down shirt, her hair blown out, and she had a perfect face of makeup on. She smiles at me as I saunter in, wearing one of Jay's oversized shirts and a fresh head of tangles piled high.

"Mornin' sleepyhead."

I smile weakly as I help myself to some coffee. I glanced at the clock on the microwave. 8:23. I close my eyes and breathe in the steam from my cup, as I walk blindly to the breakfast counter.

Jean sets a bowl of oatmeal and sliced fruit in front of me, and kisses the top of my head. "Gotta go into town and run some errands, check in on the clubhouse. Blue's outside if you need anything, baby girl. Oh, Vince called. They're running ahead of schedule... might be home early. Call me if you need me."

I raise my cup to her in silent appreciation and farewell, as she heads out the door 8:25. I put my oatmeal in the fridge, and head back to bed with my coffee.

Sometime around ten o'clock, I creep out of bed and get dressed. I throw my hair up into a clip and select the barest amount of makeup to make me look presentable. I have to rummage through my unpacked overnight bag to search for my lip gloss. A white bag sits atop of the inner contents, blocking my view.

I find my lip gloss and tuck it into my pocket. Opening the bag, I take out the bottle of prenatal vitamins and read the directions before opening the safety cap and removing one tablet, swallowing it dry. I put the bottle back in the bag and take out the Plan B package, setting it down on the vanity counter. I decided not to take the pills sometime around having dinner with Jean the other night. The seventy-two hours had expired and the pills had lost any value, anyway. Popping the pills out of their foil bubbles, I rinse them down the drain, and toss the package in the trash basket.

I reach down, spreading my palm over my abdomen. Well, the only thing left to do now is wait. I apply a thin coat of gloss to my lips and pucker into a tissue before turning on my heel, and head out for the day.

******

Sunny's Place is a large storefront on Maple Street, across from the post office. When Tiny and I were kids, it was an old-fashioned-type candy shop. We would ride our bicycles down here and clean the place out, returning home with an intense sugar high. The owners, a lovely old couple, had closed the business and retired to Boca some time ago, leaving the space vacant. Tiny scooped it up and the brothers put most of the work in while remodeling it for Sunny. The main, oversized, gumball machine was transported to Tiny's basement, and I caught a glimpse of the cotton candy machine in Jay's garage. Nostalgia is a funny thing. I mean, bikers looking for a candy fix?

The main area is light and airy, with a coffee bar and reception desk. Magazines spread themselves over a large center table, and flat-screen televisions buzz with muted, junk reality shows. The music is turned way up and the employees are roaming about, working on their clients.

Sunny is carrying a pile of folded towels from one of the back rooms when she spots me. "Fantastic... you're early. Come on, I've got a crazy day ahead and can use the jump start."

She drops the towels and beckons me over to the sink station. I don a traditional vinyl beauty cape, and sit down. Sunny is a well-established hair dresser and has shampoo girls working for her, but she comes to my sink herself and starts to lather my hair in a delicious-smelling, expensive shampoo.

She's all decked out today, resembling a 40's pin-up girl, with dramatic hair waves and bright red lipstick. She may not shampoo too many heads these days, but she hasn't lost her skills. Wringing out my hair and toweling it dry, she clips it up, turban-style and leads me to her chair, front and center of the design area.

"Hmm...," she concentrates while combing out my tangles. "I see lots of layers, and I think we should add some deep auburn."

I trust Sunny's expertise, and put myself in her capable hands. Two hours later, I had been colored, highlighted, cut, dried, and waved. It was a shame to waste such a gorgeous blowout on a regular day. Even Jay isn't around to see her work. Sunny wasn't exaggerating about her busy day. I stuck around and tried to make myself useful, sweeping up clumps of cut hair, restocking the coffee bar supplies, and answering phones.

Teenager after teenager piled in with mom in tow, to be styled for the prom later tonight. Chisolm high isn't large by any standards, but they manage to pull out all the stops for the kids on prom night. It was most certainly a black tie affair, and these girls are sparing no expense on their appearance tonight.

The nail stations are full, pedicure chairs turn over quickly, and the makeup counter is a flourish of excitement. Sunny has five other hairdressers working just as feverishly as she is. I call up the local luncheon and place a delivery order for the ladies. The last thing Sunny needs today is someone passing out from over exhaustion.

Having a moment of reprieve before the next set of chores, I sit at the reception desk and check my phone. Two messages. One from Jay, and one from Emily. I check Jay's first.

**JAY: RUNNING AHEAD OF SCHEDULE...
DON'T KNOW FOR SURE BUT MIGHT
BE HOME EARLY**

He had sent it about five hours ago.

**ME: K. GIVE ME A HEADS UP WHEN U
KNOW
MISS YOU**

It had seemed like ages since Jay had ridden away on his bike, but in actuality, it had only been just under a week. A longing swells in my chest. Looking to distract myself, I open Emily's message from about an hour earlier.

**EMILY: JULIA!! SO- T.J. CALLED ME...
DID YOU GIVE HIM MY NUMBER?**

146

Guilty as charged. Damn right I gave him her number. I knew she was too shy to do it herself, and hadn't picked up on the many clues he was giving her the other night. He's a sweet guy, and she needs a little harmless fun in her life. She lives out everyone else's love life, and it's time she starts to concentrate on her own.

ME: YUP... HE PRACTICALLY BEGGED ME ENJOY!

When the last of the teenagers has been pampered and coiffed, we lock the front door and collapse in the leather couches, reeling from the whole ordeal. Sunny looks beat-up, slipping out of her wedge sandals and putting her feet up. I hand her a cool bottle of water, which she accepts graciously before glancing over the salon. It looks like a damn tornado had hit. Her eyes widen, and then close in defeat.

I rummage through the front desk and close-out the computer, placing all of the cash and credit receipts in a deposit envelope. Marching over to Sunny, I hand it over to her and order "Take this and go home to soak in a bath. I'll watch over the girls, and we'll lock up when we're done."

Sunny puts up a very weak argument before conceding. She slips on a pair of foam pedicure slippers and heads out to her car. The daylight starts to dwindle, and it's been one long crazy afternoon.

The girls clean quickly, stocking for the following day, and power down the salon in no time at all. A cute little brunette sets the alarm and locks the door behind us as we set out to our respective homes, and the relaxation that awaits us.

I pull my little Prius out into traffic, heading west, windows rolled down, and the cooling dusk breeze passes by. The limo in front of me is packed with teens, arms waving out of the sunroof, and music pumping loudly.

I grin at the sight. Prom night is magical, and these kids are about to have the time of their lives.

THEN

I stared at my reflection, pulling and tugging on the dress in awkward places to try and settle it perfectly over my frame. Jean was bending down, placing my shoes in front of me, offering her outstretched hand as a balance while I stepped into them. My hair was curled and pinned up in a very intricate array of cascading tendrils, with a tiny, sparkling clip, tucked in for embellishment.

I nodded in the mirror to myself, "I don't know ma, do you think it's too tight? I mean what if I want to dance?"

Jean stood behind be and beamed over my shoulder at my mirror image, "It's perfect. You look beautiful, baby girl. My son is one lucky young man to be on your arm tonight." She gave me gentle hug, careful not to mess my dress. "Let's go, the car's here."

I took her arm as she helped me down the hallway. The dress was much tighter than any I've worn before, and I knew it was pretty tasteful compared to some of the others I had seen when we were shopping, but the last thing I wanted was to trip and land on my face in front of the people waiting downstairs.

My bedroom was on the second floor, and we took the steps slowly, one at a time making our way to the landing. Butch's house wasn't big compared to most, but suddenly the staircase seemed to stretch for miles.

My pop was still in jail, serving out the last few weeks of his sentence, and I was disappointed he couldn't be here to see me tonight. I could hear the voices downstairs, filling the rooms with laughter, and love. My dad may not be here for me tonight, but the rest of my family had sure made up for it.

Vince called out first as we touched-down on the main floor, "There she is! Our little baby girl all grown up." I beamed with pride. I had never felt as beautiful and special as I did in that moment. Jay stepped through the front line of well wishers and held out his hand to me. Letting go of Jean, I let him pull me into him.

"You look amazing baby," He whispered into my ear as he held me.

The many people around us cheered and joined in loud celebrating. I pulled back nervously at the spectacle we were making in front of our family. Tiny was sitting down in a chair close to the entranceway. I saw him try to stand, and made my way over to him to settle him back down before he stood.

He was still weak, only having been released from the hospital a week ago. Jean and I, as well as the other Ol' ladies, were taking shifts at his house nursing him back to health. My mom had phased-out of the picture again, once Tiny was considered stable. I hadn't spoken to her since her outburst in the hospital. She probably didn't even know it was my prom that night.

Tiny's color looked much better, but his eyes were still a little cloudy from painkillers. "Sis, you look stunning. You look like grandma, right now."

A tear started to well, as I took in his words. My grandma had been beautiful and elegant, even modeling a little bit before she settled down with gramps. I was especially close to her while she was alive, and she was my namesake.

I sniffled back my tears and laughed to mask my sadness. "You're gonna make me ruin my makeup, you big jerk."

Tiny winced in pain slightly as his chest heaved from laughing. Carol, Dewey's Ol' lady rushed to his side to tend to him. Jay called my attention back to him, opening a clear plastic case with an exquisite corsage inside, matching my white silky dress. He fumbled nervously, trying to attach it securely around my wrist.

"Case of the jitters, hmm boy?" Clink called out from the rear, followed by raucous laughter from a few of the guys. Jay looked at them and snarled, causing their laughter to increase. He then looked at me, shyly putting the finishing touches on my wrist.

Vince swooped his arm up, calming the crowd, "All right, let's get these kids to their prom, yeah? Everyone fall out."

One by one, the brothers headed out to their bikes in full riding gear. Each Ol' lady was fully decked out, wearing her rag, stating the name of her Ol' man under the curved arched words *Property of*.

Tiny was helped into the van, or cage, at the end of the processional. The doctors wouldn't be clearing him to ride yet for at least another month or so. Jay and I were the last two to follow behind. He paused to look at me once more. "Lil's you take my breath away right now."

"I love you too, Jay."

He kissed my forehead at my words, before taking my hand and leading me to the limo at the front of the caravan.

Jay's tux blended in to the dark night around us. He swore up and down that I wouldn't catch him dead in a monkey suit while we were planning prom, but here he is, as elegant and dapper as any man I've ever seen. He saw me inspecting his attire, and leaned around spreading his shoulders to give me a full view of his back.

Embroidered into the back of Jay's tuxedo is a replica of his patches. I closed my eyes and laughed. "I wouldn't expect anything else, baby."

Jay stood proud, helping me into the limo seat. "Just keeping it real sweetheart." We pull out down the street with the entire club following behind on their bikes, and Tiny pulling up the rear in the cage.

Prom was magical, beyond any expectations I could have had. Jay was pleasant enough to my friends and their dates, and even managed to dance to some of the slower songs with me. We hadn't spent much time alone in the last month or so. Every waking moment that I was not in class, I was either at the hospital or crashing at Tiny's house taking care of him. Jay brought us food and tried to distract me in the rare moments when I was able to relax, knowing that Tiny was being well cared for by the other Ol' ladies.

Since his initial declaration of love on that horrible night, we made sure to repeat it often. He was so patient and supporting, but Tiny was his best friend and club brother. I know he was just as scared and nervous as I had been. He was careful not to show it though, acting as my rock.

The prom was winding down, and couples were making their exit. Many had gotten hotel rooms on premises, and we had been invited to more than a few afterparties. Jay politely declined all of them, and I was grateful. I hadn't been alone with my man for weeks, and I needed to have his undivided attention tonight. The brothers had managed to drop off Jay's bike earlier in the night, and we had dismissed the limo shortly after dropping us off. My dress may have been a bit tight, but at least it wasn't poufy. I was able to hike it up mid-thigh and straddle behind Jay closely while he drove us home to his house.

My hands were exploring the front of his shirt, thankful for the warm flesh. My mom's words were not lost on me and I had more than a few nightmares in the time since, of Jay lying in Tiny's place, unconscious and gripping on to life with the aid of machines.

But this man in front of me was alive, and strong, heart beating loudly under my palm. He reached down and took hold of my hand, raising it to his lips before kissing my fingers, tracing just the right amount of suction behind. My exposed legs were now burning, with the heat coursing up to their apex. I closed my eyes and counted down the seconds until we were in front of Jay's new home.

We managed to dismount, and scurried into his main door in record time, kissing and groping our entire way up the walk. Once we reached the door, Jay was not letting up on his grip around my waist, to rummage for his house key. He pressed me into the oak barrier behind me, as he blindly tried each key on his ring, kissing me deeply as he carried on until he had found a match.

The door swung open behind me, causing me to sway with the sudden loss of my backing. Jay steadied me, and picked me up as he walked through, kicking the door closed behind him. He turned in the direction of his bedroom and forged ahead, gripping me tightly and staring into my eyes.

He playfully tossed me down onto his bed and leaned over me, resting his weight on his hands. "You make my heart hurt so much, I think it's going to burst sometimes, Lil's."

He rested his chin against his chest and breathed deep, hiding his eyes from mine, ashamed at his admission. I shimmied up to him, nudging his chin up with my own. "Yeah? Well you make me feel like I never thought possible." I kissed him gently twirling my tongue around the opening to his lips. "Show me you love me, baby," I asked him. "I need to feel it".

I reached up to his collar and fumbled with the top button as he stared in awe at me, flashes of need and lust crossing between us. My fingernails were longer than usual, and I was having no luck with his shirt, when he crashed his lips down to mine and let out a deep moan. Raising his hands near mine he gripped at the fabric and tore his shirt wide open, letting the buttons fall to the floor. My breath hitched at the feeling of power he was exerting, pressing down to me, guiding me to the softness below.

He managed to slither out of his undershirt without breaking much contact between our lips. I threw my head back and cried out as his hands then moved up my outer thighs greedily, settling on the elastic of my panties. Kissing and licking my neck, he let out a primal growl into my skin as he pulled his hands down sharply, taking my underwear with them. I gasped deeply before Jay covered my lips with his once more, plunging his need and strength into my mouth.

"Roll over baby," he grumbled through his breaths.

I slowly eased over onto my belly, closing my eyes at the rawness to his voice. I felt the mattress lift as he stood next to the bed and heard the shuffling sounds as he stepped out of his pants. I closed my eyes tighter, concentrating on my breathing. I had never felt this way with Jay... he was in control, expertly maneuvering his way around my body.

He slipped off each my shoes with a flick of his finger, and then straddled me, bending over to kiss the back of my neck. I tried to angle my head to catch one of his kisses when he nibbled on my ear, "Stay still baby."

A hot surge of magma plunged from the heat his breath left on my ear, straight down to my aching center, which was now throbbing in delightful mini-

155

spasms. I did as I was told. I held still, fighting against every fiber of my being not to reach around and grab this man's lips to mine.

Jay continued to trail his kisses down my back, grasping onto the back zipper of my dress and lowering it in an agonizingly-slow manner that made my body shudder. His tongue trailed behind, following the zipper's abandoned path down my spine until it had reached the end, near the small of my back. He then planted a deep kiss right above my cleft and pulled hard, yanking my dress down over my thighs. I convulsed at the sudden movement and Jay chuckled into my skin, satisfied of his effect on me.

He managed to shimmy my dress past my legs and into a heap on the floor. His hands massaged my ass checks deeply, moving down to my thighs with a deliberate urgency growing in their movements. Once they had reached below my knees, Jay put a large amount of pressure pushing and sliding them up below me so that my hips were now raised in the air.

My eyes rolled back, trying to brace myself for whatever was coming next. Jay spread my knees with his palm and then used a finger to race down my slit, barely touching it.

He moaned, "Oh God, baby. You're so wet for me."

And with that, he slammed his mouth into me, licking his way from my front to my back. I cried out loudly and grabbed on to the sheets around me as he suckled on my folds, tugging gently on the outer lips, and slithering his tongue over the hardening tissue at the top of my sex. I whimpered when he set his mouth upon it, which seemed to excite him more. He latched on, sucking and milking it with growing intensity as I squirmed deeper and deeper into the mattress with my top half. His hands were massaging me, spreading me, allowing him deeper access to my core. His groaning only added vibration to my already sensitive areas, and I felt a warm flood of heat burst under his tongue as I started to shake and cry out to Jay. My world was shattering around me, in the most delicious way.

He moved his lips to my inner thigh and continued to gently kiss, waiting for my ecstasy to slowly subside. I collapsed fully, deflated with sheer exhaustion. Panting heavily, I tried to bring myself back from the edge that Jay had just thrown me over.

Sensing my calmness, Jay nipped lightly at my thigh. "Baby... I love to make you come for me."

I nodded my head silently, void of all words. All I could muster was a deep purring to show my appreciation. Jay leaned on his knees and guided my hips to turn over for him, with my body following. He was raised above me, staring at me under him with a proud look of longing. I reached up and kissed his top lip, then his bottom lip parting my way through to his warmth. My saltiness had covered his mouth, fueling the building level of eroticism between us.

157

He held my head, splaying his fingers through my hair while gently setting me back down. Moving between my legs he urged my hips apart settling himself, bracing his weight as not to crush me. He leaned forward, deepening our kiss as he slid gently into the slickness of my folds. I whipped my head at the sudden surge of pressure entering into me. Jay guided my chin, so that I would face him again, and paused his movements

"Baby- look at me. I need to see you when I take you."

I nodded, scared at what was growing between my legs causing a sweet edge of curiosity begging for the pain that was withholding itself from me. Jay kissed my lips. "I love you Lil's."

I cried out as Jay held me, kissing my forehead, my cheeks, as he entered me fully spreading my tissues to accommodate his massive self. A lone tear dropped down my cheek from the stress. Jay kissed it away and stayed perfectly still waiting for my muscles to calm from the sudden intrusion. My pulse slowed and my body settled into its new state. Jay stared into me, eyes full of fear that he had caused me any pain.

I kissed him. "It's OK baby. I'm OK."

He exhaled and relaxed his overly tensed body, brushing my cheek with his fingers. "Lil's, I'm so sorry baby...."

I moved my hips slowly into Jay, showing him that I had recovered. "Please, Jay. Show me."

Jay's eyes lit up, the guilt melting away. His hips slowly led out of mine, leaving a strange void behind before he slid himself back into my depths. I moaned deeply with each of his movements, trying to keep up with the slowly increasing pace.

The slickness between us guided Jay as he buried himself over and over, just a little bit deeper every time. The growing tension deep below my pelvis had returned, bringing a torturous ecstasy behind it, waiting to be released. I clambered at Jay's back, desperate for him to unlock the building sensations, my nails digging into his shoulders pushing him into me.

Jay slipped his hand down between us and began to rub the tip of my opening gently, then more forcefully as my cries began to grow. He broke our kiss and called out. "Come with me baby."

I exploded into sweet jolts of release, holding on to Jay, afraid I would break apart at any moment. He was holding onto me just as eagerly, shuddering and shivering from his own release. We lie still for what seemed like a long while, unable to move, to let go of each other. We had just given ourselves to each other completely. This man now had every piece of me, owned me fully. My eyes fluttered as I rested against him, his heartbeat lulling me into the purest most peaceful night's sleep.

NOW

SUNDAY

I stretch my legs out, pressing my neck deep into the pillow, willing my eyes to open. There's nothing but darkness in front of my closed lids and I know that it's either extremely late, or very early. My inner voice is sending messages to wake, and I ignore it long enough to hear the slight sound of breathing coming from the side of the bed.

My eyes fly open and I jolt up, struggling to adjust my eyes to the shapes in front of me. The bedside lamp turns on with its dim wattage flooding over every surface as I blink hard to rid my view of the cloudiness.

Jay is sitting in the side chair, pulled up close to his side of the bed. I smile at him instantly, not recognizing the stiffness to his form.

"Hey baby," I yawn. "When did you get home".

I pull the covers back and start to crawl over to him, when he puts his hand up in an abrupt stopping motion.

"Don't".

"Huh?" I'm baffled. "OK... You just gonna sit there and watch me sleep like a stalker?" I banter trying to lighten the thickening mood.

Jay sits back in his chair and stares at me, a coldness behind his hooded eyes. I'm too tired and too confused to play games at this hour. "Baby, you gonna tell me what's going on, or are we gonna have a staring contest?" I wink to add emphasis.

Jay reaches over to the nightstand, and tosses something over to me. It lands on the bed near my knee. I pick it up and hold it close to my eyes, struggling to read the letters in my state of half-sleep.

The words finally make themselves clear. PLAN B.

FUCK. I close my eyes, and drop the package as if it were burning. "Jay, it's not what you think."

"Really? Tell me what I think, then," he spits at me.

Jay had not risen to his position in the club by being a gentleman. I know I'm dealing with a very different person than I was used to seeing. He saves this side of him for club business and hides it carefully. I know that I need to move forward very cautiously.

"Baby," I start when Jay flashes me an evil scowl at the sound of my words. I clear my throat, and start again. "Jay... I didn't take them, I swear."

Jay laughs coldly. "Seems to me the pills are missing, Lil's."

"I know," I whisper. "I flushed them down the drain and then threw away the package. I-I had a change of heart and decided not to take them."

I seem to have peaked Jay's attention. "Really?" he drips with sarcasm. "Let's say I believe you *sweetheart*.

161

Let's say you had a 'change of heart'. That means you were at least contemplating it at some point. You were gonna kill my baby and not even tell me."

He stands now, angry, and peering over the bed like a giant. "That is if you didn't actually take them anyway."

I stand up on my knees now, growing angry at his accusations. "I told you I didn't, and I meant it Jay. I had the opportunity to take them if I wanted to, and don't you dare criticize that choice until you're actually the one who has to make it. We've been apart for two years and I had no idea what was going to happen between us. But, I couldn't do it. I won't even know if there was anything to take a pill for. Not for another few days or so, anyway. The Doctor gave it to me as a precaution."

I can see his face contorting.

"A precaution... a FUCKING PRECAUTION!" he bellows. "Really? You bailed on me once Lil's, nearly killed me too. Then you come stumbling back into my life and I'm stupid enough to take you back, put my fucking neck on the line for you, without once thinking of PRECAUTIONS. And this is how you repay me? Tell me something, Lil's? Would it really be that terrible having my baby inside you? Or were you trying to run from that too?"

I slap him hard across the face. He just stands there with a blank look, gritting his teeth together.

"You ever hit me again baby, you make sure you knock me out cold or get a good head start running."

I freeze. I had never even so much as touched Jay when I was angry. I had seen what happened when some of the other Ol' ladies went after their man. I swallow hard, but my sense of resolve sets back in.

I march off to the bathroom and grab the bottle of prenatal vitamins, before turning and throwing them at Jay's feet. "This- this is hardly called running, you asshole." I screamed. "I made a mistake, OK. I let others tell me how it was going to be between us. I had doubts and fears that we were going to turn into my parents. You hurt or dead, and me an angry, bitter, old woman that hated you for putting me second. When I saw you with that tattoo girl, it just confirmed every last fear I had." My eyes tear up now, but I keep going.

"I was WRONG. I know it, OK? I'm gonna have to live with it for the rest of my fucking life. But I thought this could be a new beginning," I hold tight around my stomach. Jay's eyes drop to my center. "I don't even know if this is anything... but if it is, then it's a part of you and me. A new beginning, a way to pick up where we should have been to start with."

I drop my hands and collapse my shoulders, spent from my outpouring of emotions. "I was going to tell you. As *soon* as I knew for sure, I was going to tell you. I promise you that. I know you don't have much reason to believe me, but I swear on all of my love for you, it's true...."

I break down, giving into the tide of feelings unleashing themselves from my soul. Jay walks over, slowly pulling me into his embrace and holding me, trying desperately to quiet me down.

"Shh. Baby, it's OK. Calm down Lil's," he kisses my cheek as if I were a delicate porcelain doll about to shatter.

"It's not OK. You don't believe me. You hate me."

Jay pulls me out to see his face. "Lil's, I could never hate you. I tried. I tried so fucking hard to hate you when you left. I couldn't do it. I loved you then and I never stopped loving you, baby." He pulls me in close, rocking me. He takes a deep breath. "I believe you. You tell me you didn't do it, then I believe you."

I stand back in awe, utterly shocked. "You... you do?"

My tears slow. Jay pushes himself into me, kissing me deeply, conveying to me in touch what I couldn't believe in his words. I pull at him, claw at him, needing him to be closer. Our mouths move frantically over each other. Jay hitches my nightshirt up and grabs at my hips, swinging them up around him.

My hands move wildly through his hair, then down his shoulders, pulling and tugging at his leather vest. We crash into the mattress unwilling to let each other out of our grip. Jay throws off his cut, followed by his shirt as I hastily pull at his belt.

"Easy baby- don't want to go damaging the goods now." He helps himself to the belt buckle, proficiently opening it and letting his jeans drop to his ankles. I look on as his perfect penis springs free, offering me the comfort I so desperately seek. Jay watches as my hooded eyes follow his manhood. "Tell me what you want, Baby. Tell me what you need."

I look at Jay's beautiful, lustful eyes, and pool my courage. "I want you to make me come. I want you inside me, and I want to scream your name."

Jay smiles devilishly. "Your wish is my command."

He slams into me hard enough to make me jolt back, rebounding from the intensity. He gives me no time to recover before he's plunged himself deeper and deeper, holding my knees apart with one hand as he plays me thoroughly with the other. He strokes and presses and rubs in just the right places, to send me wheeling as I cry out to him, my orgasm shaking through me. He reaches down to kiss my lips as I come back down to earth.

"Better baby?"

I'm positioning my response when he tosses me aside, grabbing at my flimsy night shirt and throwing it behind him. He crawls into the bed after me and grips my hips.

"Just getting started baby... ride me, ride me hard."

He leans back onto the mattress and gently slaps my thigh, encouraging me to straddle him. I lower myself slowly, taking him inch by inch until I rest firmly on his thighs. I moan with the full sense of satisfaction that only his dick can offer me.

Jay reaches up to knead my breasts, gently. I throw my head to the side and call to him. "Baby... I need more."

I start to raise myself faster and faster, needing him to hit that precious spot. Jay grabs my hips firmly and digs them down into his, maximizing the force. I whimper, and Jay lifts me slightly, concern filling his eyes.

I want more and try to free myself from his hold, to fill myself again. He holds me still, in an iron-like grip. "Baby... you OK? Did I hurt you? I don't think we should be going so deep...."

His eyes move to my stomach and his hands instantly follow, massaging lightly around my middle. I reach down for his hand and raise it, opening my mouth and taking his long finger in, in just one stride, closing around it and sucking from base to tip before gently nipping the top.

"More," I command.

Jay flies into action, rolling us over so he's on top of me, pinning me down. He holds my hands above my head and uses his weight on his arm to push and thrust himself over and over again into me. I bite my lip, trying

166

to control my building need. The headboard slams over and over into the wall, setting a rhythm for Jay as he keeps his stamina strong. His groin rubs me in just the right way, with every plunge into me. I start to pant, labored uneven breathing as the deep tingling starts.

"Now, baby. Come to me now!" He calls out as I scream my pleasure aloud with his own scream to follow. Jay rolls off of me and pulls me into his arms. He tucks me into his side and spreads his embrace wide, covering me with his large hands. Neither of us speaks. We just lay in silence, our fingertips trailing circles on each other's flesh until we fall asleep.

CHAPTER TEN

The next two days are filled with the comings and goings of club members taking private meetings with Jay. They're careful enough to leave the house, either wandering in the back yard or holing up in the basement so that I won't eavesdrop. I had never been one to spy outright, but I've never missed an opportunity to conveniently stumble upon a clandestine conversation, either.

Tiny brought brought Sunny with him when he ventured over, and we managed to occupy ourselves in the boys' absence. Jay was preoccupied and quiet during meals and before bed. On the second day, I had needed a break from the uneasiness and decided to take a long soak in the tub.

The candles are lit, the bath oil added, and the lights dimmed. I stretch out, fully submerging myself under the rim of water. Jay enters the master bedroom, calling out for me.

"I'm in here, babe," I swirl my toes, having them peak through the water.

Jay walks in on me soaking in the bath and grins. "Such a hard life you have Lil's, make room."

I'm pleasantly surprised at his invitation. Jay has been attentive enough, with more than the occasional kiss or pat on the ass, but it's clear that something is weighing on his mind and I had given him the space that he needed to work through it.

Jay steps in the tub and sits behind, settling me back to lie on his chest as our legs intertwine themselves, mindlessly.

Our fingers lace through each other's and he holds on tightly, an unspoken apology for distancing himself since his early return from the club's run the other day. I bring our joined hands up to my lips and kiss a trail down his wrist, "Penny for your thoughts."

Jay exhales, but says nothing.

"Fine," I say stubbornly. "Don't tell me. I get it, I'm just a chick... couldn't possibly understand the complexities of the world around me."

Jay begins to nuzzle the top of my head. "You know that's not it Lil's. It's club shit. No need for you worry about anything, unless I need you to."

The water tickles, filling the microscopic crevices between our bodies as his chest below me raises and settles with each breath.

"Does it have anything to do with why you guys came home early?" My investigative skills had managed to pick up that something had happened on the road, causing them to end the run early. I also heard the Slayers mentioned more than once.

"Lil's... I won't tell you again. You don't need to worry about that side of things. You just concern yourself with this, with us." His arms wrapped around my stomach and he kisses my neck. "Any idea yet?"

I clasp my hands on top of his. "Not yet. I thought I'd take a test soon. Get an answer, know for sure...."

Jay massages over my skin, first my belly, my hips- then in between my thighs while lulling over my ear.

"Baby, how 'bout I do an exam to check?".

I playfully smack his wickedly wandering hand, "I don't think we've ever played Doctor before baby. Should I be a naughty little nurse or a sweet little candy striper?"

Jay slides his finger down between my opening, allowing the hot water to flood through my passage, sending a shudder down my legs. He's pinned them tightly to the sides of the tub with his own and continues his sensuous message. I moan and arch my back against him, relishing in the pleasure he provides. His one arm holds me tight around my waist as the other strokes me until I unravel around him, listless and spent.

"God, I love you baby," he hums out as we settled down, enjoying each other's closeness.

My fingers start to prune by the time we decide to go to bed, the heat from the bath draining all extra energy from us both. I wrap a towel around myself and leave the bath area as Jay blows out the candles before following me, collapsing in a heap between our bedding.

I nuzzle in close to him, bare skin on skin. "I'll have to give you a rain check, baby. I'm totally spent."

Jay laughs "Go to sleep, Lil's"

******

FRIDAY

The knocking wakes us instantly. Jay reaches over into his nightstand and pulls out his handgun, releasing the safety and engaging the first bullet into the chamber. He holds his arm out across me and instructs, "DO NOT MOVE until I come back."

I nod, pulling the blankets higher over my nakedness from yet another night of lovemaking as I watch Jay slink down the hallway. The knocking grows more intense before Jay opens the door and yells at the late night visitor.

"What the FUCK! I could have shot you, Pop."

I scurry over to my dresser and quickly dress in stretch leggings and a t-shirt, making my way to the bedroom door. There are hushed voices coming from the kitchen and I strain to listen.

"Everything OK, Jay" I call out to the men.

"It's just my pop, baby. Go back to bed. I'll be there soon."

Point taken. This is not exactly a social call and I'm being asked to make myself scarce. Crawling back to bed, I lay still, waiting for Jay. I keep an eye on the

172

alarm clock until I can no longer hold my eyes open, as exhaustion sets in and takes over.

I wake to find myself alone, no signs of Jay or Vince. I wander out to the kitchen to stumble upon Jean sipping coffee with bloodshot eyes, fumbling through the paper, reading about that schoolhouse that burnt down.

"Hey ma, Jay here?" I ask half-heartedly, fully aware that they must have left in the dark of night.

Jean shakes her head "No, sweetheart. Some shit went down last night. The boys are trying to settle it before it gets out of hand. Jay asked me to stay here with you until they get back."

I look at Jean intensely, longing for her to clue me in. I understand Jay wanting to keep me out of club business, but I'm starting to get scared, not knowing what's truly happening.

"Ma... is it bad?"

She reaches out to me, taking my hand. "Nothing they can't handle, baby girl."

Jean has probably been through nights like this more times than she cares to remember, but I'm dangerously close to a meltdown.

She pats my hand and attempts to cheerfully distract me. "Why don't you take a shower and we'll head to the clubhouse and wait for them. Pack a small bag in case we get stuck there." She smiles, trying to mask the hidden meaning... things could turn to shit and we might need to lock down.

I nod, taking in the information. I shower quickly and dress in jeans and a tank top. I rummage through my bathroom drawer searching for my necessities. The early pregnancy test box sits unopened next to my vitamin bottle. I swallow hard. I can bring it with me, but there's no guarantee I'll have enough privacy or spare moments to take it if things turn bad with whatever is going down. Or, I could just wait until things settle and I'm back home to take it in peace. The last time we were on lockdown, I was twelve years old and it lasted *two* weeks.

I rip open the box and hastily take out the contents. I skim over the directions and pop the cap off, taking the test as quickly as I can before setting it down on the counter and moving into the bedroom to finish packing. The box states that it needs to sit for two to three minutes. I'll have to check it later.

I have a few changes of clothes packed and decide to pack a bag for Jay. I doubt he had thought ahead to pack some things, as he and Vince left in a hurry. I'm checking things off of my mental packing list when my phone rings. I run to it, hoping and praying it's Jay.

"Hello?"

"Jules? It's Emily."

I exhale in disappointment. "Em, I'd love to talk but I'm in the middle of something. Can I call you back?"

There's a slight pause. "Um... actually I kind of need your help." Something is very wrong. Emily has a desperate edge to her voice that I have never heard before.

My fingers grow cold as I hold the phone. "Em... tell me where you are."

Emily is sobbing now. "I--I don't know where I am. They won't tell me. I was trying to surprise T.J. I drove to Chisolm to meet him. I saw some biker guys on the side of the road and thought they would know him, tell me how to get to the clubhouse. I followed them to some building and now they won't let me leave. They started to ask me questions, and that's how they found out I'm your friend...."

A lump forms in my throat. I close my eyes tight.

"Em... stay calm. Is there someone there with you?" I hear Emily's voice shake as she tries to answer. "OK. Put him on the phone, Em."

The receiver rustles as her phone is being passed along. "Well, if it isn't my lucky day."

SHIT. I had heard that voice taunting me, teasing at me as I waited to find out my own fate, not knowing that Jay was coming to my rescue.

"Shade." I snarl.

"Didn't think we were on such informal terms, Madame. But there's always time to correct that."

I hear Em screaming in the background. "Don't do it Julia... whatever they say, don't." Emily can't finish

175

her sentence, as the strike is loud enough to vibrate through the phone.

"SHUT THE FUCK UP, YOU BITCH!" Shade calls out to her.

Adrenaline is coursing through me, my body now on high alert.

"Don't touch her, you sick piece of shit. She has nothing to do with this. What do you want?"

His voice is practically slithering around like a venomous snake. "Funny you should ask that darlin'. Seems your Ol' man has been coming down pretty hard, getting in the way of my business." His voice drips with filth. "How's about we make a trade and you take her place while we finish negotiations with your little bodyguards?"

My head spins. Should I call Jay, tell him about Emily, risk her getting hurt in a situation she would never have been in if not for me? "Fine... where?"

Shade proceeds to give me instructions on where to meet them on the outskirts of town. I am to come unarmed, alone, and they will make the exchange letting Emily go. If they suspect that I've crossed them, he makes it very clear that they would hurt her and then kill her.

I put my phone in my cross body bag and grab my keys. I search the night side table for a pen and quickly scribble a message to Jay.

Opening the bedroom window, I climb out, pulling it shut quietly behind me and sneak around front to my car. There are two bikes parked out front, but no riders in sight. Blue and T.J. are undoubtedly inside with Jean, waiting to escort us to the clubhouse.

I climb into my Prius and start the engine quickly, peeling out and speeding away before I can be followed. The directions I had been given are leading me to the old side of town where the many factories, once the lifeline of Chisolm, now stand abandoned and decaying.

My phone rings loudly, breaking my concentration. I hesitate before answering, wrestling with myself. I can't betray Emily now, I'm her only hope. I answer the call.

"WHAT THE FUCK ARE YOU DOING LIL'S?" Jay's voice booms.

I search for words, some sort of explanation that won't compromise my friend. "I'm sorry Jay, I have to go. I have no choice... she's there because of me."

It takes him less than a second to respond, "What are you talk-"

I hang up as I reach my destination, eager to see Emily off to safety.

******

The building once served as some type of manufacturing plant. Most of the windows are broken and Mother Nature has long since started the process of reclaiming the space. I am escorted into a main foyer area by two large, unbathed, members of the Slayers MC.

Emily is tied to a chair, gagged, wriggling around at the sight of me. I rush over to her and hold her close, searching around the room, assessing my surroundings.

"Can't seem to stay away, now can you little girl... seems like you always find yourself in trouble." Shade walks out of the shadows, evil blanketing over his once handsome face. "Some might say you keep bad company...."

I stand in front of Emily, shielding her with my body. "We made a deal. I'm here, let her go."

Shade nods to one of the men sulking nearby. The man moves forward to Emily, cutting her free of her wrist ties and gag. She gulps for air, rushing into me, holding tight.

"Jules... thank God."

I hold her embrace briefly before pulling back. "Em... you're going to get out of here." I hand her my bag and car keys. "Take my car. Go back to my house. Sit tight, I'm so sorry this happened to you, because of me."

I push Emily behind me and in the direction of my car, willing her to leave quickly.

178

Shade interjects. "Well, actually...."

I shoot back at him. "We made a deal... I take her place, you let her go."

Shade smiles eerily at me, "I did say that now didn't I?" He suddenly grows bored, and waves his hand as if shoeing a fly. "However, I didn't say that my brothers here would let her go."

I gasp. Time seems to freeze as I whip my head around to face Emily, look in her widening, confused eyes. The man who had moments ago freed her from her restraints has now withdrawn a pistol from his vest and aims it at Emily's delicate head. I watch her eyes close in preparation for the inevitable. She's fully aware of what is happening.

The shot rings out and Emily's body jolts as the impact tears into her temple. Her body buckles and crumples-in on itself, falling to the ground. I start screaming and sobbing relentlessly as I watch my friend lie in a pool of growing liquid. The emotion is too much. The sorrow, the pain, the hatred, the helplessness. I collapse, a never ending fall, as my mind shuts down, leaving me to the mercy of my captors.

CHAPTER ELEVEN

JAY

I'm racing as fast as my bike will tolerate, using my mind to will it to go faster. I had left Pop and the boys behind miles ago, speeding past them, unable to keep position on our way to the hospital.

The police scanners had picked up activity from the old industrial park. An abandoned car, a woman shot... she had been airlifted to Mercy General.

I can't allow myself to think the worst. I've lost Lil's once and am not about to loose her again. I need to stay strong. I always need to be strong. FUCK. Self-hatred fills my mind. I should never have left her. I should have taken her to the clubhouse myself instead of letting her sleep, sending ma to bring her.....

Lil's had snuck off about two hours ago, right through their fingertips. Assholes. Good-for-nothing prospect pieces of shit that can't follow the simplest of instruction. Thank God I had been nearby when they called to tell me that she sped off.

What the fuck was she thinking? She didn't make any sense on the phone. We searched the house high and low for any signs of what the hell was going on. Nothing. Just a scrabble of a note and a twist in my heart.

The pregnancy test was left out, confirming what I had known for days. She was pregnant. She's pregnant with my baby and she took off for some reason. It didn't make any fucking sense. Maybe it's the fucking hormones making her crazy.

The hospital lane splits off, veering right. I race up to the emergency room entrance, weaving my way through traffic. I cut the engine and jump off my bike, throwing my helmet aside, running through the main lobby looking for anyone who might work here.

Some guy in a white coat steps into view and I run over to him, pulling on his arms. "You've gotta help me. Please, my girl's been shot. She's just been airlifted here...." His eyes are blank, void of all emotion before I can even finish my plea. Oh God, no.

The asshole cleared his throat. "I'm sorry... there was nothing we could do. She...."

I take off running through the double doors into the emergency ward, searching for my girl.

"LIL'S!" I call out around every corner, into every room, and behind every curtain. A middle-aged woman dressed in a nurse's uniform comes toward me with her hands up.

"Sir-- sir... calm down. You can't be in here."

I toss a metal cart over, grabbing my hair. NO FUCKING WAY! No way am I losing her again, not like this. I can't lose *both* of them.

"Please sir, let me help you... I can help you."

She can help me. Yes... yes. I need help to straighten this out... she can help. I let her touch my arm guiding me to her desk. I take the seat she offers me. I need her help.

An elderly security guard comes running through, but the nurse holds up her hand to him. "Jimmy, it's all right. Thank you. I can handle it from here."

The guard steps back, but cautiously eyes me. I swear to God, he comes near me I'm gonna fuckin' break his neck, right here in the middle of the goddamned emergency room.

"Sir, who are you looking for?" The nurse calls out to me, drawing my attention back to her. I watch the guard from the corner of my eye.

"My girlfriend, my Ol' lady... she was airlifted here with a shot wound." I state matter-of-factly to her, knowing that once she knows who I am looking for she can help straighten this out.

The nurse types on her computer. "Let's see... we had a gunshot wound brought in earlier by Medevac. She was unresponsive, but was identified as Julia Kaegan, aged twenty one years old, brown hair, brown eyes. She was found with her personal belongings and her vehicle was nearby."

She stops suddenly, staring at her screen. "I'm so sorry... she was pronounced dead on arrival by the attending physician."

The room grows cold. I sit stone-still staring at the back of her computer. This can't be happening. She was pure, she was innocent. None of this shit was ever supposed to touch her. All the fucked up shit I've done in my life, I know I don't deserve her. But I love her and I swore to protect her. God no.

She's so young... she has so much to live for. She'll never grow old with me, she'll never get to hold our kids and grandbabies... SHIT. The baby.

I close my eyes when the realization hits that if she was lost then the baby was lost. "The baby," I let out, hanging my head in defeat. This was it. There was nothing left for me.

The nurse types on her keyboard, hitting buttons over and over again. "Sir... there was no baby. The patient wasn't pregnant."

I lift my head in confusion. Everything swirls around me a million miles an hour. "What? Yes she was.... I saw the test myself."

The nurse double checks her computer screen. I pull the screen over to see for myself, as she jumps back, startled.

A hardening resolve sets in, "I need to see her."

******

The morgue is in the basement of the hospital, with the service elevator being the only access. I had to lie to the administration and tell them that Lil's and I were married and I was her next of kin to gain entry. I had left strict instructions for no one to disclose anything about her to anyone until I could make sure it was real.

Something just didn't sit right. You find yourself in as many close call situations as I have, you learn how to trust your gut. Sometimes it makes the difference between life and death. I had to sign too many forms and grow impatient with the small spectacled man in front of me.

I grab his collar, a full eight inches below me. "Just show me the fucking body."

The little pencil-pusher drops his clipboard quickly on his desk and leads me over to a wall of drawers. Pulling on a large handle, the door opens with a plastic covered body expanding before us.

My baby can't be under here. I would know, I think, if she were gone. Like some kind of invisible cord between us snapping, severing the connection I have always felt with her. If I am wrong, and this is her, then at least I owe it to her to see what I'd done. This is my fault, this is on my shoulders. I couldn't protect her.

The employee puts on a pair of white gloves and carefully lowers the plastic. I close my eyes. I had seen a lot of shit in my life. Hell, I had done worse to people than what was now before me. I can do this. I need to do this.

I open my eyes and move over the young girl lying before me. I turn on my heel and head back to the elevator. There's no time to waste.

The gloved man calls out to me, curious about my sudden departure. "Sir, If you'll just please sign her release for the mortuary."

I turn in the open elevator, pressing the red button. "Don't have to... That's not my girl."

TO BE CONTINUED IN BOOK TWO
<u>A LIL' LESS LOST</u>
AVAILABLE NOW ON AMAZON.COM

Please be kind and leave a review for the book you've just read

ALSO FROM THIS AUTHOR:
BABY V
BOOK ONE IN THE CHIANTI KISSES SERIES
PLEASE ENJOY THIS SAMPLE:

PROLOGUE

The definition of an arranged marriage:

Marriages in which family members take a significant role in bringing a couple together. Relatives, particularly parents, often take the initiative to find, evaluate, and approve potential spouses for their children.

CHAPTER ONE

The church bells finally finish chiming but I can still feel their metallic vibrations course through me. At least I will *never* have to hear those god awful bells again. Ever. Four years of listening to the slightly off-beat tolls have been enough to drive me to loathe them on more than one occasion. In the beginning, they were charming... that lasted all of a week. Soon after, I could sense the daily noon ringing like a well-tuned internal alarm clock, as it usually meant that I was late for class. If I was *really* lucky, it meant only that my rare, but desperately needed afternoon nap was about to be interrupted. I know I'm not alone in my lack of affection for the old bells, because whenever anyone refers to them... it's always as the "damn bells."

I look around at all of the other girls lined up with me and wonder if any of them are thinking the same thing about that last ringing. It was just another one of those "last" memories we would all share before graduation. Our last exam, last night in our out-dated but charming dorm rooms, last assembly-line styled breakfast, and our last days as students at St. Bart's. Until today, we had all been heading down the same path. In about two hours, we would splinter away into a hundred or so different ones.

"Well, do I?"

I snap out of my daze with a confused "Hmm?" to my right.

"V... do I look like I have too much lipstick on? I want to be able to see my lips in the pictures, but not to look like a cheap pin up doll. Christy says I have too much on. I don't think I have too much on. Do I *really* have too much on?"

And this is the last time I would have to listen to Katherine Lang ask me one of her mind numbing questions.

"No. It's not too much. The photographers are like ten feet away from the stage and I don't think they're taking close up shots." I really have no idea what kind of photos they were going to take, but I probably wouldn't have worn as much of the pale pink lip lacquer that the petite blond slathered on herself.

Thanks to the inescapable alphabetizing of last names, I have had to endure random questions like this for the last four years. I look down the line of endless burgundy gowns toward the coveted "T" section of the group with envy. Stephanie catches my eye, giving me an overly enthusiastic and sarcastic thumbs up.

I would give anything to change my name right now. Nothing too crazy... something generic like Tate or Thatcher will do. But *nooo*. I'm a Lombardi and stuck with the "L"s for just under two more hours. I hope.

I don't think this can last longer than that. Father Cross is known to give a long-winded Sunday morning sermon but even he wouldn't want to stand out here in the blazing sun any longer than he has to.

Before I can finish rationalizing the merits against a drawn out graduation day, the familiar orchestrated beginning of "Pomp and Circumstance" begins to play loudly. Taking a deep breath, I follow Katherine's lead toward the stairs of the newly erected stage. As I grab hold of the bannister, I stand tall on my toes to try and see out into the crowd.

Hundreds of happy faces and flashing cameras are staring back toward us. Quickly glancing over the waving children, pointing parents, and people fanning themselves with folded programs, I scan for the large group of familiar faces that are waiting to see me take a seat behind the podium. I am about to give up and turn my attention toward the last step, when I find what I am looking for. A dozen or so adults and a gaggle of little kids all with the same light olive skin and dark brown hair as mine, stand out against the background. I smile knowing that my family is beaming looks of pride in my general direction.

Concentrating on the task at hand, I carefully walk halfway across the stage to my assigned seat, sitting as gracefully as I can.

Mission accomplished. The last thing I need is to trip over my tent of a graduation gown and fall flat on my face before my brothers. They would never let me live it down.

The sun beats down on us like a fry lamp at any given fast food establishment. Our gazes respectfully aim toward the back of Father Cross' head, but I'm sure I'm not the only one stealing glances of their personal group of fans every few moments.

Mine is probably one of the larger ones. Sister Mary Francis wasn't thrilled when I handed in my seat count for the ceremony. I'm sure she would have told me to trim it a bit but held her tongue thinking about the amount of zeros on my family's endowment check to the school every year.

Most of them are here today. Well, the ones living on this side of the Atlantic, anyway. Mom, Nonna, Aunt Rosie, my brothers with their wives and kids... and Theresa and Dom. I take inventory of each of them as I check them off my mental family list. And then I notice it.

"Miss Katherine Lang"

Father Cross turns slightly toward us as Kate gently squeezes my hand before getting up to receive her diploma. I smile and nod in return... chuckling a little when I notice the pink smear on her left hand. She had decided to remove some of her war paint before having her perfect smile immortalized for her graduation pictures. Smart move.

I quickly move my attention back to my personal group of troublemakers starting to share collaborative looks between one another as they sit up in preparation. This is *not* good. If the four of them are communicating through silent glances and nodding with little smirks thrown in, that means they are all thinking somewhere along the same line. I'm on the receiving end of those lines of thinking more times than I care to recall.

The applause is loud but polite for Kate. Her family makes the expected cheers with her name being added to phrases such as, "Go Kate!," "That's my sister," and "Yay Katie!" Perfectly fine, tasteful and acceptable.

She grasps her diploma, faces the small group of men with wide-angle lenses stationed below the stage, and I can imagine her flashing the megawatt but slightly plastic smile she is famous for. It's the same smile she gives everybody, every time, exactly the same. I'm sure it was perfected somewhere around thirteen years old in the company of her vanity mirror. Lipstick was probably added somewhere around her sweet sixteen for dramatic effect.

The applause dies down while Father Cross angles himself back towards the microphone perched atop of the podium.

"Miss Vincenza Maria   Lombardi."

I hold my breath and stand up, preparing for the noise.

I lock eyes with Father Cross, steadily heading in his direction. I have tunnel vision. *Just concentrate on reaching the podium and take my diploma when he hands it to me.* This is all I can think of to drown out the spectacle starting to erupt about ten rows deep into the crowd.

My eyes do not budge from that diploma as it nears. The last thing I need to do is give them a reaction. I've learned the hard way over too many years, that if they see the slightest bit of frustration or acknowledgement... then it just carries on longer.

Father Cross, headmaster of St. Bartholomew's Women's University, looks like a deer caught in headlights. I'll bet he's never had this happen in the twenty-plus years he's given this same drawn out commencement speech, handing out these leather bound diplomas. I can't ignore the touch of irony in the situation, though.

Here stands the man who time and time again refused to change the outdated school curriculum after countless petitions and student senate meetings.

Finishing and Etiquette courses are mandatory no matter the degree you were completing. After all, St. Bart's is well known to be one of the finest (and few remaining) institutions where the daughters of the upper-crust can be educated in all things "proper and polished".

With families like this seeking out their services, why would they change protocol? It isn't like the students are paying the bills or granting the ostentatious endowments. The families do, and the last thing Father Cross will let happen on his watch would be for the benefactors to suddenly loose faith in his archaic and traditional policies.

And yet here we are on a beautiful Sunday afternoon, enjoying the fruits of his labor... while the wealthiest, most financially generous family that this school has likely ever seen is making a scene the likes of which St. Bart's gentry have ever witnessed.

A very small, crooked smile is fighting through all of my efforts of suppression. It is the same type of smile this man has given me every time I presented him with the school year's latest petition to no longer mandate trivial classes such as "Traditional dance," "Entertaining," and "Social graces."

I extend my right hand out toward the deep burgundy leather portfolio he is grasping and my left hand to take his salutary greeting. Widening into a full smile, I turn in the direction of the photographers below, and the clicking sounds begin. His palm is sweaty, but cold. Weird and gross at the same time.

My peripheral vision begs my attention. They're on their feet, hands in the air, pumping. Fingers are cupped around mouths to project the hooting and hollering further, louder. My little nephew Johnny is being held up in the air to add his own voice to the mix of calls being shouted my way.

WAIT. There's a sign. Fuck. Really? A sign? I can't resist the urge any longer, and stare full-force in their general direction, taking in the entirety of it.

Mike, the youngest and most mischievous of my three older brothers (and most likely the ring-leader of today's affair), is holding up a rather large white cardboard sign with professional lettering sprawled across it... huge letters shining and sparkling in the bright sunlight.

WAY TO GO BABY V!

The blood rushes to my face before I can try and contain it. Mike is waving the sign back and forth, slowly, while doing his best impersonation of a rabid sports fan. His brown hair flops around from the sudden motion of jumping up from his seat. He sees me watching him and adds a nodding motion to his yelling.

John is next to him, holding little Johnny high above the crowd. Pure glee is painted across Johnny's ("JJ" as only I call him) round little face. As the eldest of my brothers and head of our family, John should know better than to

196

encourage the next generation to jump on the "Baby V" bandwagon. As angry as I am with him, I can't help but notice the look of pride on John as he holds his first born and only son up to watch me receive my degree.

Tony is next down the line of men making fools of themselves. His perfectly gelled coif and artificial tan stand out among the crowd of W.A.S.P.y alabaster complexions. The Jersey Shore has nothing on my brother Tony. He is suave to a fault and a killer ladies man. My inner Gloria Steinem is itching to add the phrase "man slut" to the mix, but Tony has a heart of gold and has never treated a woman badly. He treated them well in fact... *all* of them. But, he's a tamed man now, and married faithfully for over a year. Tony is so excited and laughing hard enough that he practically doubles over. Dom is slapping him on the back while laughing himself.

Dom. Gorgeous Dom with dreamy eyes. Tony was a ladies man, but he was just a wingman compared to Dom. Dom can have any girl he wants... and probably has. Growing up, all of my friends swooned over him like flies on ice cream, and he loved every bit of it. Domenico is not a blood brother to me like the other three, but close enough that I never hesitate adding him to their collective title. They are simply, "The brothers."

Dom's eyes lock with mine long enough to see his famous grin and sly smile, before he adds the loudest boast yet to the ordeal.

"Way to go, Baby V! Bring it on home!"

Before he can finish as enthusiastically as he started, Theresa elbows him hard enough to ensure there isn't a follow-up. That's my girl! Although Theresa is Dom's younger sister, she always has my back. As the only two girls in our family, we have an unspoken allegiance to each other.

Theresa has had her share of the boys' antics growing up, but, as the baby of the group... I bear the brunt of it.

Dom pretends to be injured, cowering away from his little sister while she returns her attention my way, and politely claps... just as I had done at her own graduation ceremony last year.

The two are quite a pair. For however handsome Dom is, Theresa is equally beautiful with her huge almond eyes, and long, wavy, blown-out hair. She is the closest thing to a sister as I'm sure I'll ever find.

After the full five-second timeframe perfected during countless hours of graduation rehearsal, I turn once more to Father Cross. His lip quivers a little in restrained anger as he issues his standard well-rehearsed words of wisdom.

"Congratulations my child... and God bless you."

Simple. Sweet. And probably more than a little difficult for him to say at the moment.

~*~

In a matter of moments, the great lawn has been transformed into a sea of chaos as relatives and loved-ones swarm around in search of their particular graduate. It probably doesn't help much that we are all dressed in the same identical burgundy ceremonial gown. Twice now, someone has grabbed on to me only to find that I was not exactly who they were expecting.

Maybe this will be easier if I just park it somewhere and wait to be found, instead of playing the maze-game with several hundred well dressed but impatient audience members? I head over toward the largest oak tree in the center of the lawn to relax under its shade until the craziness settles.

The temperature instantly drops a few degrees as I feel the trees relief from the brutal sun. Pressing my back against the ancient tree, I graze the crowd looking for my mom. She is the only person I want to see right now as I'm still angry at the boys for their little graduation present from thirty minutes ago. Instead, I see another familiar face walking toward me, making an audible "Tisk, tisk" sound while smiling.

"How is it that you can turn something as boring as a graduation ceremony into a small scandal?," the friendly visitor finally asks as he joins my shaded spot.

I reach out to hug him, thankful for the lighthearted distraction. He follows his chiding with a soft embrace.

"Hey Conrad. So... you saw that, huh?" I ask back sarcastically. I haven't seen Conrad since spring break when he came to pick up Stephanie to take her home. He laughs lightly in my ear before tightening his grip and whirling me around.

"Of course I did. I was nodding off, listening to Cross ramble on and on until all hell broke loose!" He gently places me back down and lets go of his grip to look at me. "So... Baby V, hmm? What's that about? I've never heard anyone call you that before. Something new?"

"No... something old. Annoying, and old. Have you found Steph yet? I saw her over by the flower garden a few minutes ago," I quickly change the topic away from my personal humiliation.

He moves us deeper into the shade. "Yeah, I found her. She's taking pictures with our parents. So, how does it feel to be amongst us grown-ups, in the real world now?"

Ha! I can barely call Conrad a grown-up. He is no more an adult than his sister or I am.

"I am officially declining to answer any such questions until after the Summer is over. I figure I can stretch out one last season before joining in the trenches," I answer back while shaking my head.

"All right...," he gives me a pass. "I'll ask you again in September, then. Enjoy it while it lasts. Steph tells me you two are going to be roommates in the city this fall?" He takes on a visibly confused exterior. "Seriously, I don't get chicks. I've spent eighteen years living under the same roof as her, and I couldn't *wait* for us to go to college just so I wouldn't have to deal with her every day. You two get paired up for four years and can't seem to let it go. I've seen how she keeps her room, V."

He rests a playful accusing finger on my chin, "You're a glutton for punishment."

I step up to defend my friend, even in jest, "Steph's not *that* messy. She's just organizationally challenged, I think. Yeah, we're going to look for an apartment downtown while we both get internships. Hopefully."

I had no idea Steph had told her brother about our plans for the fall. I scramble to think of a polite way to ask Conrad to keep it on the quiet side until we definitely have plans set, when I see him look over my shoulder, his face tensing nervously.

"There you are. We've been looking all over for you." I turn to see Dom standing a few feet away from me. His deep brown eyes looking from me to Conrad and back. "I told your mom I'd find you for pictures."

Conrad recovers from the sudden discomforting intrusion.

"This must be one of your loudly-proud brothers then? Nice to meet you," he speaks to Dom as he politely extends his hand. "Conrad Thomas, Stephanie's brother," he introduces himself.

Dom hesitates for a split-second while looking down at me. He's always been substantially taller than I am, but I somehow feel him grow in height. He reaches out for Conrad's hand and shakes it casually while maintaining his fixed gaze on me.

"No, I'm not V's brother. I'm a *really* good friend," he reluctantly shifts his eyes to Conrad. They probably should have let go of their grip, but keep it going awkwardly.

"Dominic DiBenedetto. Good to meet you. I didn't know Stephanie had a brother."

He finally releases the younger boy's hand.

The two of them can't be more than eighteen inches apart, facing each other. Dom is definitely the taller of the two, but Conrad straightens his shoulders as if to gain a few inches to make up the difference. Neither of them break their stare. I think fast to come up with something to say before this starts to become even more uncomfortable. Dom beats me to it.

"But... you see those three goons over there? Standing by the fountain, staring at you? *Those* are her brothers. I think they want to see their baby sister and congratulate her," he slowly states with a subtle hint of disdain as he places his opened palm on my lower back, adding a slight amount of pressure to will me to move with him toward where he's pointing.

"Uh, yeah. That's fine. Congratulations, V. I'll catch up with you later then?," is all Conrad can manage to speak before I am out of earshot.

"Thanks! I'll call Steph about meeting tonight. You in?," I call back slightly increasing volume as I am being led away.

He nods over-enthusiastically.

"Sure! Talk to you then!," he finishes while still standing in the same spot under the oak tree, trying to figure out what exactly just happened.

No longer trying to yell out to Conrad, I turn fully toward Dom and stop walking, placing more weight in the heels of my shoes to counter his gentle guiding. He realizes quickly that we have slowed and looks down at me, not releasing his position from its place on my lower back.

"What?," he playfully lets out while rolling his eyes. "Come on V. Are you really *that* pissed at what we did? It was Mike's idea. But it was a good one," he continues his argument. "You're the last one to graduate... we couldn't pass it up."

I exhale deeply and loudly, "You are *all* idiots, you know! Really! You couldn't just act your age and at least *pretend* to be mature for one afternoon, could you?"

I scold him as my pointed finger presses into his tie. I was expecting to push into his chest for full dramatic effect, but meet resistance under my fingertip. Dom practically lives at the gym... but I guess I didn't give him enough credit. His chest was a *lot* firmer than I thought it would be.

He moves his free hand to cover my accusing pointer finger and presses it so that my palm flattens out over his silky tie. Keeping his hand covering mine while changing his tone from one of jest to a softer, sweeter one, he begins the apology.

"I'm sorry, V. Really... I am. You know us. We bust your chops. That's all. I mean... you must have expected us to do s*omething*...?"

His brown eyes are somehow softer now, no longer laughing silently as they were before. His hand is strong on top of mine, as if he is holding it to reassure me of his words. Not wanting to brow-beat him any more than necessary as he obviously thinks I'm damn mad at him, I pull my hand back and use sarcasm to return to our usual and familiar banter.

"A sign?... Really? With Glitter! That's above Mike's planning skills, Dom. Neanderthals can't read, let alone write."

I turn on my heel and storm off toward the other three idiots about to feel my wrath.

LIKE WHAT YOU'VE READ? BABY V is
available on
AMAZON.COM

About the Author

Tara Oakes is a new author from Long Island, N.Y. She lives with her husband and their little pet family. She is an avid reader, a DIY'er and writer of all things romance. With several completed works, _A Lil' Less Broken_ marks her debut into e-publishing.

When not writing or reading, Tara enjoys gardening (without much success) and all things _Real Housewives_ related. Please feel free to contact her as all feedback and fan interaction is much welcomed and highly appreciated.

Authortaraoakes.com

@Lil_Oakes

Liltaraoakes@aol.com

21502614R00126

Made in the USA
Middletown, DE
02 July 2015